Горнмир
На Службе Царей

BORIMIR
Serving the Tsars

Part One: Alexander II

by Wayne Goodman

First paperback printing, July 2018

Copyright © 2018 by Wayne Goodman

Version 1.00
1 July 2018

ISBN: 978-0-9989007-3-5
Library of Congress Control Number: 2018907064

waynegoodmanbooks

waynegoodmanbooks@gmail.com
Twitter: @Wgoodmanbooks

Contents

A STORYBOOK TALE *requires a storybook setting. St. Petersburg defied the reproach of its critics and detractors as a precariously improbable city that should never have been. Built upon the bones of laborers ordered to drain and fill the swamplands (and perched on the brink of inevitable disasters—either natural or human-caused), it fell and rose time after time. Floods, fires and violent uprisings periodically devastated the well-ordered streets, crisp stone buildings and majestic metal monuments, but like Sisyphus or the Phoenix, St. Petersburg persisted.*

It all began with Tsar Peter, who wanted to be as far away from Moscow as possible and closer to the more modern cultural centers of Europe. He feared the sinister forces in the old capital and longed for the sophistication of the celebrated ones to the west. A new version of Amsterdam—a place he had visited and admired—sparked his imagination and vision. Perhaps even a Russian interpretation of Paris or Rome.

According to legends and myths, in May 1703, Peter stood on a marshy island in the mouth of the Neva River —within visual range of the far eastern edge of the Gulf of Finland — grabbed a halberd from the hand of a nearby guard, cut two rectangles of peat, formed them into an 'X' (or Cross), and proclaimed, "The city will be here!" He then dropped the weapon, picked up a shovel and began digging the foundation for a fortress to be named (in Dutch) 'Sankt Pitersburkh,' after the monarch's patron saint.

According to historical records, Tsar Peter was nowhere near that site the day excavations began.

This tale begins when two servants of the House of Romanov meet for the first time under rather auspicious circumstances.

Section One:

An Emerald Among Rubies

February 1880
Alexander Palace Kitchen, St. Petersburg

*This soufflé **must** be perfect!*

Boris Mikhailovich, the 20-year-old son of peasant farmers had a pale, pink face with an aquiline nose, short, curly blondish hair and a pointed goatee. He broke eggs over a large, just-scrubbed-clean bowl, separating out the yolks the way Adolphe Dugléré had taught him at *Café Anglais* in Paris. There must be no trace of yolk or the albumin would not be able to retain the air he would beat into it with a large wire whisk, which he had brought back with him from Paris. He knew no such thing existed in St. Petersburg. Even if the tiniest piece of shell fell into the bowl he would have to start all over.

It would take an hour or so to prepare, and if dinner was to begin in 15 minutes, dessert would be called for about 45 minutes after the guests had been seated, giving Boris exactly one hour to finish his grand finale.

This was to be the first time he made his signature dish, *Soufflé à la Russe*, for a Royal Family dinner, and he wanted to impress his new employers. Alexander of Battenburg (the recently-elected Prince of Bulgaria and a nephew of the Tsaritsa, Maria Alexandrovna of Hesse) was to be the honored guest.

It was only a week ago that he had served the Tsar's son, Grand Duke Sergei Alexandrovich, this dessert at *Café Anglais*. Duke Sergei even made the effort to go into the kitchen with his younger male companion to meet the chef who had developed the specialty just for him. The Grand Duke then invited the young man to work in the palace kitchen, as one of their favorite cooks had just left due to pregnancy.

His recipe called for eight egg whites, and he had just completed number six when the door banged opened to reveal a stunning fellow wearing a bright scarlet, knee-length military jacket, black boots and a white fleece hat with the red crown emblem. Below the visor, Arctic-blue eyes sparkled from a pale, pink face framed by a dark-brown trimmed beard. The two men locked gazes for a slightly uncomfortable two seconds, and half an eggshell dropped into the bowl of previously untainted whites.

"Ebat," muttered Boris as he looked down into the contaminated goo.

The handsome guard, Vladimir Yuryevich, had to walk a dozen *arshins*[1] just to get out of the Palace and then a few more after that to reach the kitchen, which sat outside the main Palace, off to the side. He strutted over to the kitchen chief, Nadezhda Ivanova, a middle-aged, somewhat masculine, woman with care lines generously distributed around her burnished face. Along the way he glanced once more at the cute blond fellow washing a large bowl at the sink. Their eyes locked again, and the guard stumbled on a loose floorboard. The blond man smiled quickly but then returned to his chore.

"Nadezhda Ivanova," Vladimir's voice reverberated off the metal pots hanging from racks. He then whispered as to not cause further interruption. "The Prince's train has been delayed from Berlin. Dinner will not begin as scheduled."

The woman nodded, then turned to the open room. "People," she croaked, "the guest of honor will be late to arrive. Please halt your preparations."

Boris sighed in relief. His mistake would not cause a delay after all. He could stop blaming himself for being distracted by the handsome guard. The guard who kept looking over at him.

"Who is that new fellow?" Vladimir started to point but pulled his hand down before his gesture became obvious.

Nadezhda followed the guard's gaze and then turned back to him. "Oh, that one! The Grand Duke found him in a Paris kitchen and brought him back here to replace Ludmilla Maximova, who is with child. Apparently, he prepared a special dessert for Sergei Alexandrovich, and the Duke took a liking to both."

"He is very attractive. I can see why Sergei Alexandrovich has an interest."

"Yes, well you best keep your eyes off of the Duke's new plaything if you know what is good for you," the cook admonished.

Vladimir faced her, "And how is Svetlana Grigoryevna? Is she well?"

The woman waved a hand, "You know—or perhaps you don't—after ten years, you hardly talk."

"Nadezhda Ivanova. I am surprised at your cheek," the guard responded. "She has been very good to you."

"Yes, I suppose you are correct in that. Ten years." She exhaled heavily and raised her eyebrows. "Ten years," she mumbled as she turned back to her sack full of unpeeled potatoes.

Boris finished cleaning the mixing bowl and looked across the room at the guard speaking with the kitchen chief. "Sergeant!" he called out, waving his hand to attract the man's attention. When the object of his summons failed to respond, he shouted again, "Sergeant!"

"Oh, no," Nadezhda whined at a low pitch. "Be careful with that one, Vladimir Yuryevich, he could be trouble."

"Trouble?" he responded. "Trouble often finds me, and I have a way of handling it, Nadezhda Ivanova." As the guard marched away from the kitchen mother and toward the beckoning Boris, he added, "Thank you for your concerns."

"Sergeant," Boris started again, "I need to know exactly how long it is we are to be delayed. My dish takes one hour to prepare, and dessert is scheduled for 45 minutes after the beginning of service, so—you see—I must begin 15 minutes before the start of the dinner. The timing is of utmost importance!" he finished with a flourish of fingers and hands.

Vladimir smiled at this performance, appearing to suppress a grin. "And whom do I have the honor of addressing?"

"Boris," he announced, "Boris Mikhailovich. Pastry chef to his Imperial Majesty, Tsar Alexander."

The guard looked back at Nadezhda, who squinted and rolled her eyes simultaneously. He grinned at this but waited until his smile relaxed before facing the cute blond tempest again.

"And you are, sir?" Boris beckoned.

"Vladimir Yuryevich, sir. Royal Guard and personal body-guard to his Imperial Majesty, Tsar Alexander." He bowed slightly for effect. "So you see, we serve the very same master."

"Volodya—may I call you Volodya?" Boris intimated.

Vladimir bristled. "No. No you may not. My name is Vladimir Yuryevich, and I do not believe we are quite acquainted sufficiently for you to use such familiarity." He stared down at the slightly shorter man with the adorable curls.

Boris trembled slightly. "I did not intend offense, Sergeant, but from the way you looked at me, I assumed–incorrectly, perhaps–that…"

The guard stared into Boris's hazel eyes as if to appear menacing, but when one eyebrow popped up, and that side of his mouth raised, the charade ended. "Perhaps someday I shall call you Borya and you shall call me Volodya, but today is not that day. Now, I must return to my post, but before I do, my curiosity has infected my thinking. What dish is it that you were preparing that is so time-sensitive?"

Boris smiled, "Ah, I am glad you asked."

Nadezhda had walked up behind Vladimir during this exchange, and she elbowed the guard's ribs as she passed, as if to say, "You've done it now!"

"*Soufflé à la Russe!*" the chef expounded. "Developed at *Café Anglais* especially for His Majesty, the Grand Duke Sergei Alexandrovich, on his most recent visit to Paris."

Vladimir nodded as if he understood, though perhaps he did not. "And what is it that makes this particular dessert special—Boris?"

The chef raised his chin and pointed his face victoriously, "I use the ginger root from Tula, my family's home, and molasses to flavor the dish. It is unique!" He pointed toward heaven in an attempt to increase its uniqueness.

The guard glanced over to where Nadezhda ended up by the pantry. She shrugged her shoulders and reached for the handle just as the whole room shook violently.

A noise, louder than anyone had ever heard before, erupted from beyond the door to the kitchen. Smoke and dust blasted through the opening. Several people lost their footing and fell to the floor. Pans sprung from their racks and a table careered over.

The blast propelled Vladimir up against a wall, which kept him from falling to the floor. He surveyed the wreckage, pausing briefly at each person's face. He hesitated for an extra second on Boris's frightened eyes. "Is anyone hurt? Do you need assistance?" he shouted out.

Several grumbles filled the air, as well as a few curses. No one seemed injured, just shaken and dirty. People began to take stock of the damage, cautiously looking around at their anxious fellow workers. Another blast might be imminent.

Boris approached Vladimir. "What was that, Sergeant?"

The guard looked down at the angelic face covered in soot, the eyes a pair of emeralds staring out of the dirt. Vladimir raised his arm as if he were going to hug Boris, but the lift paused prematurely, and he merely patted the chef's shoulder reassuringly.

"All of you remain here where it is safe. I shall go determine the cause of the disruption and return with some answers," he announced to the entire kitchen staff before exiting. The others looked to Nadezhda, who had begun to clean the area and return the fallen cookware to its proper place. Boris's eyes followed the retreating guard.

The kitchen staff had no idea that Stepan Khalturin, a dissident from the political action group Narodnya Volya ("the People's Will"), had hired on to assist with Palace construction. He was able to sneak in a stick or two of dynamite each day, hiding it in a storage room. When the plans for a formal family dinner had been announced, the assassination plot advanced. Khalturin relocated the nearly 300 pounds of explosives to a space beneath the dining hall and lit a fuse timed for 18:30, the hour the dinner was to commence. As the guest of honor had gotten delayed, the blast went off while none of the Royal Family were in the hall. Several nearby rooms, including military quarters, collapsed into heaps of bricks, plaster, granite slabs, and dust. Eight staff members died, and almost 50 soldiers received wounds from the blast. Fortunately for the kitchen staff, the distance between the Palace and their workroom provided sufficient space for them not to be directly impacted by the massive explosion.

Although their beloved Tsar Alexander II had done much to advance the quality of life for most Russians, this was not the first attempt on his life. He had assumed the throne in 1855 following the death of his father, Nicholas I, who had traveled to Sevastopol with his troops fighting the Crimean War. During Alexander's reign, he made every effort to clean up the corrupt government: restructuring the judicial system, modernizing the military (after the dismal defeat in Crimea due to outmoded weaponry), encouraging local self-governance, and, most importantly, emancipating the serfs, thereby ending hundreds of years of impoverished peasantry. Even with all his improvements upon the nation's status, attempts to take his life began in 1866, when a group of disenfranchised university students acted upon radical, Socialist ideas set forth in a popular call-to-action book, 'What Is To Be Done?' Formal plans for an assassination attempt began following the execution of Solomon Wittenberg in 1878, a dissident who had been caught trying to use a mine to sink a ship carrying the Tsar into Odessa harbor.

Vladimir returned to the kitchen to find the staff still a bit nervous and fearful, working to clean up the mess from the blast. He explained what he had discovered, and several people burst into tears as some of the dead happened to be their friends and family members. Even as the messenger of sad tidings, coated with ashes, choked with regret, the handsome young guard displayed respectful compassion, patting a shoulder or two around him.

A set of hazel eyes peered across the room, "Thank you, Sergeant." A slight smile followed. In the dust on the work table, the pastry chef wrote with a finger:

БОРИС + ВЛАДИМИР БОРИМИР
[BORIS + VLADIMIR BORIMIR]

He gazed down at his creation, grinning at the way the two names interlinked, providing him with fanciful thoughts of future possibilities. But then Boris realized Vladimir, the Tsar's private bodyguard, would never have any interest in a mere kitchen worker. His hand smoothed the dust from the blast as if it were pastry flour until his hieroglyphs disappeared into the woodwork.

позже

Later that evening, in his rather spacious and comfy quarters large enough for two people, Boris sat at his desk reading and writing correspondence with his friends and family back in Tula. He needed to let people at home know that he had not been harmed by the earlier assassination attempt on their beloved Tsar.

Hours after sunset he still felt sleepless, and he decided to venture out into the St. Petersburg nightlife to calm his nerves. Extra guards surrounded the entrance, but they knew who he was and acknowledged him as he passed through the grand gate. Nearby church bells rang out the happy news that the Tsar continued to live on.

Snow patches decorated some of the sidewalks, and a fog of frozen breath formed as Boris hurried to Nevsky Prospekt, a few blocks away. Most evenings St. Petersburg was a city of night-dwellers, life after sunset flourished and blossomed under the gaslights glowing through the late evening mist.

When he reached the grand street where he had hoped to satisfy his urge for companionship, it appeared very few other people had sought out the same entertainment. The sidewalk cafés stood empty, no groups of young men arguing about philosophy or politics, punctuating their beliefs with rolled-up newspapers and tracts. Even the heavily-trafficked *Passage* past Mikhailovskaya Square proved unusually vacant and quiet.

He realized finding male companionship to ease his tensions would not be easy that night. Finally, in resignation, Boris crossed the bridge over the Fontanka River and followed the shadows to the notorious Znamensky Baths. He was no stranger to the Turkish bath, he had even been born in his village bathhouse because it was the cleanest place in town. This St. Petersburg bath would not have received such an honor; it stung the nostrils with the odors of musty Russian sweat and pungent sour cabbage.

Once inside, Boris approached the proprietor, Gavrilo. The older, grizzled fellow from the Balkans showed him a set of miniatures, each with the face of one of the attendants available. After fingering through a dozen or so candidates, Boris found just the one: a fellow who slightly resembled the good-looking but stand-offish Sergeant he had met earlier in the day.

Gavrilo nodded and told Boris to wait at the front. A minute later, a younger, leaner version of Vladimir appeared. Boris's smile gave away too much information because these lads were not necessarily inclined to pleasure themselves with other men, and if they knew you had a special interest, their price rose accordingly. "Igor," indicated Gavrilo, and Boris knew that was not the boy's real name.

Boris followed "Igor" down the main hallway to a room where the handsome, muscular fellow parted curtains to a small parlor with a tall table in the middle. The attendant indicated for him to enter, and Boris gladly stepped into the room, happy to be away from probing eyes. Steam poured from vents around the baseboard, giving the place an aura of mystery and sensuality. It did not, however, cover the pervasive stench of sweat and sour cabbage. Around him he could hear moans of pleasure and groans of delight. Some of the other patrons received rubdowns and baths, others received slightly more, depending on the price.

And the price did not matter anymore because Boris now worked in the service of the Tsar and he needed particular personal attention. He knew the routine, and as soon as the tattered curtains fell together, he began to disrobe, placing his fur-lined coat, shirt, pants, and small garments on the hooks provided. "Igor" had placed a fresh towel on the table, and Boris climbed up, positioning himself face down.

The masseur quoted a price for the bath and a price for anything else the customer might require. Boris readily agreed to both, knowing exactly what it was he required from "Igor" and how much he needed it. The bathhouse boy began by swabbing Boris's legs and arms with the hot, moist towels used for bathing. "Igor" paid special attention to certain areas that might garner him an extra tip for his services.

After a few minutes, the lad nudged Boris to suggest he roll over. By that point, Boris had become aroused and there was no hiding it. "Igor" continued to bathe his client, again paying special attention to certain areas. Once he realized the time was right, he lifted Boris's legs and placed his own aroused member where he knew it would extract a handsome gratuity. While this young man was no substitute for the attractive and swarthy palace guard, Vladimir, he was what was available to Boris in the moment. A stifled yip, tightening and relaxing followed, and "Igor" thrust deep inside, earning his money and ensuring a large tip as well.

At first, Boris felt remiss and uncomfortable with the situation he had devised. He tried to keep his eyes closed, hoping the boy would get tired and give up after a while, but with just about every thrust of "Igor's" well-developed hips, an arousing grunt accompanied the motion. After a few minutes of frustrating pleasure, Boris opened his eyes and looked up at the sweaty, contorted face of the fellow holding his ankles. When the boy opened his eyes, they were a light blue, similar to Vladimir, but not as intense. This realization propelled Boris to the brink. He shifted his own torso slightly, and with the next stroke, the well-equipped bath attendant hit the target inside, resulting in spurt after spurt from the pastry chef's pent-up reservoir.

As the bath attendant mopped the many splashes of sticky substance off of Boris's chest with a fresh towel, the chef felt the insufferable weight of the real world and realized he had to return to the Palace before it got too late. He leapt from the table and reached into his pants pocket, grabbing enough rubles to satisfy "Igor" plus two more for superior service. Boris finished dressing himself with a satisfied grin.

At the front, he thanked Gavrilo for a most excellent time, and Boris hurried along the frosty cobblestones hoping no one he knew from the Palace recognized him.

позже

The next morning Boris dashed to the kitchen a few minutes late because he had overslept. With no time for his usual morning toilet, he appeared quite unkempt, with uneven beard stubble, frowzy hair and bits of crust around his eyes.

When he stepped into the room, everyone seemed to be standing at attention because the Palace chief-of-staff, Dmitri Konstantinovich, appeared to be holding some sort of session. Sporting a shiny satin suit and matching shiny bald head, Dmitri paused when Boris entered, and his squinty, disapproving eyes followed the young man as he hustled to the proper station. An exasperated "Hmmph," passed through the chief's nostrils as his lips gathered tightly. This new pastry chef had been placed in the kitchen by request of the Tsar's son, thereby removing Boris from the usual scrutiny applied to job seekers at the Palace, and Dmitri Konstantinovich did not approve of such side-stepping procedures.

"As I was saying," the Chief-of-Staff droned, "due to the disturbance of evening last, we are short five military quarters and some of you will have to double up in your own rooms until the reconstruction is completed so that we may accommodate the guards." His head rotated on its rather narrow neck so that the gaze ended up pointing directly at Boris. "Especially those of you with luxurious staterooms."

Boris swallowed uncomfortably. Perhaps he did not realize his quarters were somewhat superior to those of his co-workers.

"Excuse me, sir," Boris began speaking and stepped forward. "I wish —"

"Yes? And you are?" the Chief-of-Staff balked in a mean-spirited manner, as if he did not to know the boy's name.

"Boris Mikhailovich, sir. Pastry chef."

Nadezhda's eyes turned heavenward. The corner of Dmitri's mouth began to twitch, the way it did when he had to take orders from Tsaritsa Maria Alexandrovna.

"And what is it you wish, Boris Mikhailovich? If it is a special request, I suggest you not abuse the staff time with your personal issues, thank you."

"No, sir, not at all, sir. I wish to volunteer to host a specific military guard, sir, if that pleases you."

Dmitri's eyes narrowed. "While I appreciate your spirit of volunteerism, I do not believe I would entertain such a request. It is my specific duty and position to make these important decisions." He turned to face the room. "Now, may I see a show of hands from —"

"Excuse me, sir," Boris interrupted, "but if you are not able to entertain my voluntary request, perhaps I could have His

Majesty, Grand Duke Sergei Alexandrovich assist you in making such a decision."

The rest of the kitchen staff shuddered and sucked air. Dmitri startled visibly. He was not used to such impertinence from staff members, especially new ones who had escaped his usual comprehensive interview process. "Perhaps, Boris Mikhailovich, we can discuss your issue in private after I conclude my business here."

"Yes, sir." While he returned to his station, his fellow kitchen workers looked at Boris more oddly than usual, and he began to wipe the crust from his eyes and tousle his hair into position.

"Now, as I was saying, may I see a show of hands —" Dmitri Konstantinovich continued over the next 15 minutes on his mission to arrange having the military guard take temporary beds in the rooms of the other kitchen staff. During this process, he gazed at Boris a few times, observing the insubordinate air and cocky smile. He also paid attention to the attractive blond's curls, boyish face and goatee.

When the Chief-of-Staff had concluded his ministrations, he bellowed, "Boris Mikhailovich! Come with me." He waggled his stubby finger, turned abruptly and strode out of the kitchen.

As Boris passed Nadezhda, he smiled, but she glowered back.

He followed the stumpy Dmitri along the concrete path adorned with marble Greek-style colonnades and trailing vines. They entered a service door of the palace and made the sharp turn into the Chief-of-Staff's office. Inside, Boris gawked at the lavish, expensive-looking appointments. An intricately-designed, deep maroon, hand-woven carpet nestled beneath fine French padded settees. A short, roll-top desk with inlaid wood occupied the area below the oval window at the rear.

Dmitri sat at his desk and indicated one of the settees for Boris. The Chief-of-Staff took a moment to further analyze the young upstart. "I am not in the custom of being addressed with such collegiality in front of the service staff."

"I am sorry sir, but I wanted to display my initiative."

"Initiative, yes." Dmitri fiddled with his fingertips. "Initiative can be good in many circumstances, but this is the palace of the Tsar, a structure of tradition and history where is no place for personal initiative. Do you understand me, Boris Mikhailovich?"

Boris merely nodded, his unwashed curls bouncing with each bob of his head.

"And I would also appreciate it if you did not hold your personal relationship with the Royal Family above my head like a dangling sword."

Again, the curls followed Boris's nodding head.

The Chief-of-Staff closed his eyes and inhaled slowly. "Now that we have the preliminaries out of the way, you say there is a particular person you wish to have as a temporary mate?"

"Yes, sir. Vladimir Yuryevich, one of the Tsar's personal bodyguards."

"Vladimir Yuryevich," Dmitri pondered, savoring the name of the handsome young fellow whose family had served for many generations. "I will consider your request," the Chief-of-Staff gritted his already ground-down teeth. "However, I cannot guarantee that your demand will be addressed as ordered."

"Thank you, sir," Boris responded.

"Now, on to a separate—but related—matter." Dmitri locked the pastry chef in his gaze. Boris swallowed painfully. "Your deportment demands some attention, young man. I do not care if you were placed in my kitchen by His Imperial Majesty himself, you must behave according to certain… standards."

Boris's head tilted to one side, suggesting his inability to understand the veiled request.

"How shall I put this," Dmitri gazed down at his paper-filled desk. "We do not tolerate particular behaviors in our staff. Do I make myself clear?"

The pastry chef continued to stare at his superior with a blank look.

Dmitri's domed head tilted back in annoyance as he took a noisy breath through his nostrils. "Why do you have to be so thick?" He gazed at Boris once again, attempting to dismiss his unbidden attraction. "We request… nay, require that the male staff act like men, not… well…" He gestured limply with an open hand toward Boris.

"If my behavior upsets you, Dmitri Konstantinovich, I am not sure what it is that I am doing to unnerve you, sir." He looked directly at the Chief-of-Staff, who immediately looked away.

"Let us just say that you prefer the company of men over women, and that sort of thing is frowned upon here." Dmitri could not face the young man now.

"I am not sure how my personal life has any bearing on my kitchen position, sir. I have not committed any criminal acts, nor do I discuss my personal business at work."

"Criminal acts?" coughed Dmitri Konstantinovich. "Have I accused you of such things? As long as you do not violate Article 995, [2] there should be no problem."

Boris held his head up with chin pointing, "Sir, I do not see any reason for this line of interrogation. I have not heard of your Article 995. How does it relate to my service?"

Dmitri swallowed a grapefruit uncomfortably. "It refers to certain conduct between certain men. When you… penetrate," the word seemed difficult to say, "another fellow for sexual pleasure, you have violated Article 995."

The pastry chef swung his head away from the Chief-of-Staff's attention. "I see. Well, I shall attempt not to violate your Article while in the service of His Imperial Majesty. Is that all, sir?" Out the window gardeners tended to the lawns around the fountains.

"Not quite. I also request that you please try not to strut about like a white peacock while you are on duty. It is most distasteful and distracting."

"Birds of a feather…," Boris mumbled to himself. He stood and started toward the door.

"Wait!" cried out the chief.

Boris halted and turned back. "What?"

Dmitri stared at Boris intently, "Your face, boy. Your face!"

Boris lowered his eyebrows at this undecipherable accusation.

"You keep clean-shaven. It is a clear indication of your proclivities, and I will not have it in my kitchen!" The blush of his own face and scalp rose quickly. "Even your *friend*, the Grand Duke himself, maintains traditional masculine facial hair, despite his untraditional lifestyle."

The pastry chef stepped toward the desk to face his accuser from above. "I believe I was hired on for my abilities in the kitchen, not my manner of grooming, sir. Perhaps I shall have to call upon the Grand Duke to discuss this particular issue." He turned to leave again.

"Wait!" Dmitri called out. "There is no need to go above my head for this, Boris Mikhailovich." He rubbed at his scalp while attempting a calming smile but achieved only an ingratiating grin instead. "You are correct in that your facial hair does not impact your performance in the kitchen. However, I expect that your personal business will not interfere with the completion of your duties. If we must have this conversation again, I shall consult with His Highness beforehand."

"Thank you, sir. And thank you for entertaining my housing request, sir."

Dmitri waved the back of his hand, "You may return to your duty now."

Boris exhaled and left, regaling in the ornate appointments of the palace hall and the garden path back to the kitchen. As he arrived, Nadezhda was in the midst of reviewing the day's schedule and menu for the family meals.

Soon after, the kitchen door opened and all heads turned to see who entered. There stood the handsome, young guard Vladimir Yuryevich, tall and seemingly at attention even though it was not required. He marched over to Nadezhda and smiled. She merely nodded her head toward Boris, who bristled in anticipation of the visit to come.

"Boris Mikhailovich," Vladimir began as he approached the pastry chef, who busily prepared pirogi for the day's meals.

"Oh, Vladimir," he looked up with mock surprised, as if he had not seen the guard even though everyone in the room could see he had. "How nice to see you again so soon." He smiled. "Is there something I can assist you with?"

"As a matter of fact," the guard whispered, "it seems the Chief-of-Staff has assigned me to sleep with you." He pointed at Boris.

"I must sleep with you?" the chef acted taken aback. "Isn't it a bit soon for that kind of thing? We have barely spoken…"

"Keep your voice down!" Vladimir did not seem to pick up on the drama Boris attempted to create. "Because of the explosion, some of the military guard are being housed with other staff members, and—for some reason I cannot understand—he has chosen you to be my host until the barracks can be repaired."

Boris halted his pastry work and looked up at Vladimir. "I see. Then I shall have to have a little talk with the Chief-of-

Staff because I cannot, and will not, share my room with just anyone. It is my personal space, and I find this totally unacceptable!" He chopped the table top with his flattened hand. Some of the other workers giggled at this gaudy display.

The guard peered down at Boris with the hint of a smile. "That is quite interesting because—you see—my quarters were not affected by the blast," he spoke in a hushed tone, "and there was no reason to move me. Apparently, someone requested that I be placed in your room, Boris Mikhailovich, and I think we both know who that someone might be." He grinned his enigmatic grin again.

"I saw the way you looked at me when you first entered the kitchen yesterday," Boris protested. "I think we both know what that means, sir!"

Vladimir's Arctic-blue eyes smiled at the suggestion and he touched a finger to his lips. "I'm not sure exactly what you might think it meant, but I intend to follow my marching orders nonetheless. I shall arrive with my belongings this evening after the Tsar has taken to his bed." He started to leave but then turned back, "And you could do with a decent shave." Vladimir stroked his own smooth cheek for effect.

Thankfully, Boris did not have a knife in his hand at the time. Otherwise, he might have unintentionally cut off a piece of his finger. He looked up to the guard, "And what time might you be arriving, sir? I usually turn in rather early."

"Really?" Vladimir suppressed a smirk. "I believe I saw you leaving the Palace last night rather late. I went to your room and knocked. No one answered. Perhaps our ideas of 'rather early' differ quite significantly."

Boris turned his head away, "I could not sleep after the traumatic events of the evening, and I went for a walk to calm my mind."

"To the *Passage*, no doubt." Vladimir whispered the word '*Passage*' as if it were the day's secret password.

The pastry chef faced the guard with a look of surprise. "And how do you know about the *Passage*, Sergeant? It does not seem the type place someone like you would know about."

Vladimir looked around to see if any of the others happened to be listening. Their heads snapped dutifully back to their work. "I know quite a bit about our beautiful St. Petersburg. One does not spend his whole life in a city and not know such things."

"Well, if you followed me, Sergeant, you saw the *Passage* was completely dead last night and I ended up going to Znamensky —"

"Gentlemen," Nadezhda shouted, "please take your interview outside. This is a place of work, not a coffee house where university boys argue over the state of things!"

"I apologize, Nadezhda Ivanova. It was improper of me to conduct such an interview here, and I shall return to my post now," Vladimir stated. He turned to Boris, "And you, my new friend, I will see tonight. Please make every attempt not to upset your superiors in the meantime." An about-face and strut to an unheard military cadence propelled the guard out the door.

"Tonight..." murmured Boris.

позже

The hours could not fly quickly enough for the young pastry chef. During the afternoon, military officers visited the kitchen to observe the damage caused by the previous day's blast. Each room of the Palace received its own scrutiny to ensure nothing like that ever happened again. While it was somewhat disruptive to have a straggling stream of strangers parading through their workspace, comfort could be drawn from the sense of increased security. Knowing that their beloved Tsar remained the target of the very people he had tried to assist weighed heavily upon the Russian souls of the Palace staff.

Once the Royal Family had finished their evening meal, and the kitchen cleaned, Boris headed back to his room in anticipation of the events to come. On his writing desk he found a few letters waiting for him. One in particular, from Alexander Borodin, caught his attention. A mutual acquaintance, Vladimir Stasov, the impresario and critic who supported many of St. Petersburg's artists and composers, had organized a concert to help their old friend, composer Modest Petrovich Mussorgsky, raise some funds for living expenses. He had been fired from his civil service job the previous month (some say he only had to show up and breathe to receive his salary) and had run out of money (most of it spent on cheap Vodka). Stasov had gone through the composer's correspondence and sent these notices to everyone he found.

Boris had met Modest Petrovich a few years prior at a Bacchanalia he attended soon after reaching Paris. Mussorgsky had undone his shirt, and he flounced about the room, hair like a thistle, wriggling his fingers in ecstasy as he danced from person to person following rhythms of unheard music. People shouted at him, giving him suggested poses to adopt: a faun, a nun in ecstasy, Napoleon. At one point he halted, facing Boris directly. Neither of the two men knew the other, but the composer studied the young man's face intently for a few seconds before bursting out, "I shall take two of this one!" He grabbed Boris's shoulder tightly as the assemblage laughed on. "Does anyone have a match for him?" People roared with laughter as Boris froze, not knowing how to conduct himself in the situation. Modest Petrovich reached into a coat pocket with his free hand, drew out a cigarette case and queried the room, "Does anyone have a match for me?" The crowd burst into hysterics at the antics of the famous man.

The claw-like grip eased as the older fellow smiled upon the face of the younger. "So fresh, so innocent. If only I could make you mine." He walked off in a grey cloud of despair, leaving Boris standing amidst a throng who converged upon him. "Ah, men…"

"Did you know who that was?" one of the other party-goers asked. Boris just shook his head. "Only Modest Petrovich Mussorgsky, of course! One of your best Russian composers!"

The next day, Boris received an invitation to visit Modest at his Paris hotel, which happened to be on the next street over, next to *Palais Garnier*, where Mussorgsky's opera *Boris*

Godunov enjoyed a month of performances. Given the chef's busy schedule at *Café Anglais*, he had to decline the offer but invited the composer to dine at the restaurant. The next evening, Mussorgsky and his entourage of noteworthy admirers dined under the ministrations of the famous Adolphe Dugléré. When Modest Petrovich inquired regarding Boris, explaining he was the sole reason his party dined in that particular establishment that particular evening, the head chef sought out the young man from the kitchen and brought him to the table of dignitaries. From then on, Dugléré spent more time with young Boris, imagining him to have other important, impressive and wealthy friends.

Following this episode, Boris and Modest kept up irregular correspondence, until a few months back when the composer's life descended into a dark abyss of alcoholic excesses.

Just as Boris considered reaching for his diary to determine if he was available the evening of the benefit, a set of authoritative raps sounded on his chamber door. Rather than display any eagerness for the arriving guest, he continued to sit at his escritoire, with his back facing the door, trying to respond as calmly as he could muster. "Enter."

Boris heard the door open behind him and the rhythmic clacking of the guard's boots on the polished, parqueted wooden floor. "You should not do that," admonished Vladimir.

"Do what?" Boris turned to face the intruder while still sitting in his chair.

"Sit with your back to the door and ask a stranger to enter. That is how people get assassinated, you know."

Boris stood, still holding the letter from Borodin, and looked at the guard directly. "Yes, I imagine it is your job to protect important people from their enemies. However, I am not an important person as such, and, as far as I know, I have no enemies."

Vladimir closed the door behind him and set his valise down. He had changed out of his Royal Guard uniform at the barracks and now wore a belted, grey wool kaftan. "Perhaps you are correct, Boris Mikhailovich, in that you are unaware of your enemies. However, we all have enemies, sir, whether we know it or not."

A chuckle escaped from Boris, "I would be very surprised to learn that I had any enemies, Sergeant."

The guard performed what appeared to be a quick visual survey of the spacious, luxuriously-appointed room. "One is usually unaware of his enemies until it is too late, I am afraid." His eyes stopped at the beautifully-crafted Chippendale chair on which Boris sat.

"You sound like a suspicious, overly-protective guardian, Vladimir Yuryevich."

Now the guard chuckled, "It is my exalted position to perform those precise duties, my friend. I am one of the personal bodyguards to His Most Excellent Emperor of Russia, King of Poland, and Grand Prince of Finland, Tsar Alexander Nikolaevich Romanov." He bowed and saluted.

"Where are my manners?" asked Boris as he waved the letters about in the air. "Please make yourself comfortable." He stood and placed the piece of paper atop a growing pile of correspondence.

"What is all that?" Vladimir pointed at the papers on the desk.

"What is what?" replied Boris, looking about, trying to determine what it was the guard did not recognize.

"All of those papers on your table there." He pointed.

Boris looked at his desk. "Oh, this?" He turned back. "I keep correspondence with my family back home in Tula, and I have many friends in Paris and here in St. Petersburg that I write to almost every day."

"That sounds exhausting," Vladimir offered. "How can you keep up with all that social interaction? It must take hours."

"An hour or two—every evening—but well worth it, I assure you." Boris now appeared a bit puzzled. "Do you not write your friends and family, Sergeant?"

"I have no family, sir. They have all died in the service of our Tsar. As for friends, I see them every day on duty and there is no need for me to be writing correspondence to them." He stared back at Boris.

"That sounds utterly dreadful! Having no friends or family to correspond with." He lifted his goateed chin slightly. "I would be lost without having my letters every evening."

"It appears you and I lead very different lives, sir."

"Indeed, but now we have to share one very small room until your quarters are repaired."

Vladimir laughed. "I would not call this a small room. No, not in any measure. It is twice as large as the one I usually sleep in—along with three other people!"

Boris looked around, "I am sorry, then. I had no idea my room was so superior to others." He also took note of how nicely the belt of Vladimir's kaftan accentuated his masculine physique.

"Well," the guard responded, "when you are a personal friend of the Grand Duke, you receive special attention."

"What are you speaking of, sir?" His eyes popped open.

"Are you not the 'special friend' of His Imperial Highness, Sergei Alexandrovich?"

Boris's jaw fell. "What are you saying, Sergeant? I have no relationship with the Grand Duke, 'special' or otherwise. Where did you hear such nonsense?"

"Your kitchen boss, Nadezhda Ivanova, suggested that you are beholden to His Imperial Highness."

"No, no, no!" Boris stomped in a little circle. "That horse of a woman most likely has a penis larger than mine! And she certainly has the eggs of a man." As he pronounced the word 'eggs,' Boris cupped his crotch in a rude gesture. "The Grand Duke invited me here to make pastry, nothing more!"

"It appears His Imperial Highness might think of you as a bit more than just a pastry chef, sir." Vladimir waved his arm about the room to indicate the special status provided.

"Well, I do not know what to say to your ungrounded accusations, Sergeant! I requested no special treatment from the

House of Romanov. All I wanted to do was prepare my exquisite pastries for them." Boris locked heated eyes with the guard, and for a few intense seconds, neither of them blinked or looked away. "I am truly sorry," he finally had to turn his head, "to hear about your relatives."

"There is no need for your sorrow. We have lived in the service of the Royal Family for over 100 years. I have never known any life other than that of the Russian court. It has been an honor and a pleasure to serve our country's rulers." Vladimir stiffened, almost to attention.

"And I come from a long line of poor, country peasants. I have had no connection with royalty in my life until now. How silly of me to believe that all the other servants had similar quarters."

Vladimir raised his eyebrows, "Yes, how silly of you." His gaze locked upon the other's face. "And you still require a shave." Boris glared back at him. "But where am I to sleep? I see only one bed in this rather large room."

"One bed, yes, but I believe it is big enough for two to share," Boris raised his eyebrows.

"Was it not you who protested that it was too early in our acquaintance to sleep together?" Vladimir grinned. "Perhaps I should sleep on the floor for now until I can requisition a folding cot or some other temporary bed."

"Yes, perhaps you should." Boris smiled to himself as he returned to the writing desk. "You can stow your belongings there," he indicated a marble-topped dressing table with deep drawers.

"Thank you, Boris Mikhailovich." He opened the valise and surveyed its contents. "Or may I now call you Borya?"

"As you wish, Vladimir Yuryevich." Boris picked up the letter from Borodin and began to peruse it while his new roommate organized his belongings with a bit of a smirk.

"What is that you are reading now?"

"Hmm?" Boris looked up, turning the paper in his hand. "Oh, this? It's an invitation to a piano recital on the weekend to help a friend who has recently lost his job." An idea struck him. "Do you fancy piano music, Sergeant? Perhaps you could join me."

Vladimir smiled slightly. "My mother used to play for me when I was a child. Glinka, mostly." He nodded with nostalgia. "Yes. Perhaps it would be a good opportunity for you and I to spend some time together away from this Palace."

"Excellent! It is settled then. I shall inform my friend, Alexander Porfiryevich, that we are planning to attend. Now please excuse me while I finish my daily correspondence." He sat at the desk shuffling papers around, barely able to keep his mind focused on reading and writing.

While Boris pretended to continue his correspondence, Vladimir pretended to continue unpacking his belongings, neither looking across the room at the other. After about a quarter of an hour, the guard had arranged some bedclothes on the floor near the dressing table.

"Good night, and thank you, Boris Mikhailovich," the dark-haired man uttered as he lowered himself to the ground.

"Yes, a good night to you as well," the blond absently responded. "You are most welcome. Most welcome."

позже

Vladimir woke to the sound of metal tapping on porcelain. He had been dreaming about the feel of raspy, blond bristles on his own smooth-shaven face. When he opened his eyes, he saw a pinkish pair of feet about one *arshin* away, and he realized he was lying on the ground. Recalling what led up to sleeping on the floor, a night or two of this uncomfortable abasement seemed like adequate penance for the gift bestowed upon him from Providence the previous day. Through a veil of glaze, he observed Boris hacking at his face with a razor, attempting to remove a few days' worth of beard stubble. At the all-important chin, the chopping converted to short, sharp strokes, as the pastry chef was careful not to remove the goatee, to which he seemed particularly attached.

When Vladimir coughed unexpectedly, Boris gazed down and smiled enigmatically. "Good morning to you, Sergeant." He then returned to his morning toilet.

The guard stirred himself from the floor, realizing how stiff some of his joints felt. Perhaps more blankets tonight would provide a warmer surface. Once he managed to stand fully, he placed himself next to Boris and looked into the mirror. It would take but a few minutes to prepare for the day's duty. However, as he considered the relative position and likeness of the two men, it reminded him of a photograph he had seen of his own parents. How he resembled his father, Yuri Vladimirovich, proudly wearing his service military uniform. The softer, smoother, angelic face of his roommate was not as close a match for his mother, but the difference in heights seemed similar.

"Sergeant, if you please," Boris requested. "I must prepare myself for the day."

"Yes, Borya. I am sorry. I did not intend to impede your progress." He stepped back, giving the pastry chef more space. "By all means."

"Thank you. I shall finish soon and you may have your time at the basin, sir."

At hearing Boris address him so formally, "sir" and "Sergeant," Vladimir winced. "And, by the way, I believe it would now be acceptable for you to address me more personally."

"Ah," responded an amused Boris, "I may now refer to you as Volodya?"

Vladimir winced again, "Well, not exactly. Volodya was my grandfather. If you wish, you can call me by the name my mother used: Vovka."

Boris smiled with delight. "Vovka it is!" and he returned to his preparations. "And my mother used to call me Borushka, but Borya is acceptable as well."

"Borushka," Vladimir muttered to himself. "Yes, I believe I prefer Borushka, particularly if we are going to remain intimate for the period of my temporary relocation." He peered sidelong at Boris, who appeared to be smiling at some personal thought.

Vladimir stood watching Boris as he continued to chop-chop away at his face. As one of the Tsar's personal bodyguards, it fell to him to groom His Imperial Majesty from time to time. He would use slow, gentle strokes to attain the closest shave. The chef must have learned his annoying hacking method in France.

"Oh, Borushka," Vladimir remembered something he wished to ask.

"Hmmmm?" Boris thrummed while shaving cautiously at his chin.

"When is this charity concert to be? It is possible I shall require permission from my superior to attend if it conflicts with my scheduled duties."

"Yes, of course." Boris walked to his desk and searched for the letter from Borodin. "St. Petersburg Conservatory of Music, this Sunday, 16:00, which I guess will give the church-goers time. Suggested donation, one ruble, but no one shall be turned away."

"Thank you." He looked down at his crumpled underthings. "His Imperial Majesty attends military roll call on Sundays, but it generally finishes in time to be back here well before we would need to leave. I shall enquire today."

Boris wiped at his face with a towel and then twirled it away with a flourish. "There! Finished. Your turn—Vovka." He smiled at saying the name.

"I shall use the facilities at the barracks, but I appreciate your hospitality." He bowed slightly, and he espied Boris taking advantage of the opportunity to study the guard's nearly-naked form. Vladimir drew on his kaftan, cinched the belt, and strode to the door. "Until this evening, then. Thank you for housing me." The guard grinned with a hint of maliciousness, "Even if it is just temporarily." He opened the door and stepped out into the hallway.

When Vladimir reached the barracks, his cohorts whistled and winked at him. "Did you *sleep* well, Vladimir Yuryevich?" "Is he a good kisser, Vladimir Yuryevich?" "Did you eat his pastry, Vladimir Yuryevich?" his mates teased and taunted.

"Enough!" shouted Vladimir. "Borushka slept in the bed and I —"

"Borushka! How cozy!" The others laughed at Vladimir's discomfort. "You had better keep your hands and your thoughts to yourself, friend. The Grand Duke might not take kindly to you mishandling his playthings." Again, they laughed at Vladimir.

Instead of reacting or responding, he moved to the toileting area and began to prepare for the day ahead. Once he had donned his uniform, he walked to and knocked on the door of his superior's office.

"Yes? Come in."

Vladimir opened the door and peeked inside, "Sir? May I speak with you?"

"Of course, Vladimir Yuryevich." The Lieutenant of the Guard, Alexei Andreyevich, stood behind his desk. His stature was shorter than Vladimir, but somewhat wider. His gruff smile peeked from beneath a wiry, greying mustache.

Vladimir stepped into the office, closing the door behind him. He stood before the officer's small, wooden desk and saluted. "Sir, I wish to request leave this Sunday after we return from troop inspections."

Alexei Andreyevich placed his palms on the desk, supporting his heft as he returned to a sitting posture. "You know, His Imperial Majesty prefers you by his side. It is quite an honor, Sergeant."

"Yes, sir. And it is my preference to guard His Imperial Majesty with my life at all times. However, there is a social function this Sunday afternoon that I would like to attend with a friend."

"I see." The lieutenant rifled his fingertips across the desktop. "Would you like to have the entire day at leisure? I can find a replacement for you if you so desire?"

"Oh, no, sir. It is my pleasure to accompany His Imperial Majesty on roll call. I know he is quite fond of the ritual. I only wish to have the afternoon to myself."

"Perhaps His Imperial Majesty could accompany you to your social function, Sergeant. Is it something he might enjoy?"

Vladimir coughed into his hand. "Sir, it would be a great honor to have His Imperial Majesty accompany us, but I will be attending a charity concert for a poor friend."

"Of course. Nothing that would interest His Imperial Majesty."

"Besides, Lieutenant, the concert is scheduled for the Conservatory of Music, and the building does not allow for adequate protection of our Tsar."

"Yes, I see." The squat man stood slowly. "Of course you may have the afternoon for your enjoyment. I believe this to be the first time you have requested any personal time at all, Sergeant. This must be an activity of some significance."

"Not really, sir," Vladimir scuffed his boot on the flooring and looked downward. "My roommate invited me to go with him, and I was hoping to spend more time with him in an effort to build camaraderie."

The Lieutenant peered at the Sergeant with a slight squint. "Is this the little pastry chef from the kitchen? I have heard talk of your association with him."

"Yes, sir. Is that an issue?"

"No, not at all," he waved a hand in dismissal. "I have heard that he is here at the discretion of the Grand Duke. Please keep in mind that the safety of our beloved Tsar is paramount." A pudgy finger poked skyward. "Paramount!"

"Yes, sir. Of course, sir. Thank you, sir."

"Dismissed."

Vladimir walked back into the barracks room expecting further taunting from his comrades, but they had all left and reported for their various duties.

Throughout the day, his mind kept wandering to the decision he had made to go to the concert with Boris Mikhailovich and requesting the time away. Up until that day, he had always served his appointed hours and duties.

What has changed? Had he changed? Had circumstances changed?

The family of Vladimir Yuryevich had served the Tsars for generations. Each new son would find his place in the Royal Household following graduation from military school. He had been fortunate enough to attend the Page Corps at Vorontsov Palace, paid for by the Romanov family.

Hundreds of years before, Vladimir's family had land, serfs and minor titles. They appeared at court and held audience with the Tsars. Then a long drought followed by economic setbacks drove them into service of the House of Romanov directly. And now, generations later, Vladimir Yuryevich continued his ancestors' roles by serving their esteemed Tsar.

A few times, during his short recesses throughout the morning, he entertained the idea of going over to the kitchen building to say hello to Boris Mikhailovich. However, he reasoned that too many visits from him might seem overly generous and familiar, and he did not wish to create more problems for either of them.

позже

During the mid-afternoon, Vladimir happened to be passing near the door to the kitchen, and he saw Nadezhda Ivanova outside, leaning against the wall.

"Are you feeling unwell, my friend?" He approached her, observing the visible amount of sweat on her forehead.

She puffed a few breaths before looking up. "Ah, Vladimir Yuryevich! What brings you to our outpost here? I think I might know the answer to that, so you need not answer." The kitchen chief laughed a few hearty guffaws but then doubled over, coughing violently.

"Nadezhda Ivanova! What is happening?" He did not know whom to call for help, but he looked around and found no one nearby.

One hand firmly against the wall, she pulled herself upright again. "No, no. Not to worry, Sergeant. Just an old lady who has worked far too long for far too little."

Vladimir studied the woman's pallid face for any clue to her health status. "Perhaps I should send for Svetlana Grigoryevna."

With sudden agility, Nadezhda Ivanova came back to life, vigorous and smiling. "No, please, no. She would only worry me to death! I just needed some fresh air. And—by the by—your friend the pastry chef has gone to the market for supplies. Apparently, the kitchen of His Imperial Majesty is lacking when it comes to proper ingredients." Her facial expression, eyes raised to the very top and a pouty mouth, indicated her growing dislike of the new man in her kitchen. "I can only hope your interactions with him instill a proper sense of place. He behaves as if he is the only one with any experience, training, and taste." She poked the guard with a finger.

"Yes, Nadezhda Ivanova, our young friend has much to learn about serving in the Imperial Palace. I believe that you and I will be able to devote some time and attention to this situation, yes?" He smiled both at his old friend the kitchen chief and his other, new friend, the absent pastry chef.

"Until later then," she turned and opened the door, but stopped before going through, "And this will be our own private conversation, yes, Sergeant?" She touched the side of her bulbous nose with a crooked, witch-like finger.

Vladimir touched the side of his own nose and nodded. As he walked back to his duty post, he whistled what he remembered of "The Hut of Baba-Yaga" from *Pictures at an Exhibition* by Mussorgsky.

позже

That evening Vladimir returned to his shared room with Boris after the Tsar had taken to bed. As before, the blond baker sat with his back to the door, in contrast to what the guard had advised.

"I see you still prefer to invite misfortune by allowing your enemies to sneak up upon you," Vladimir taunted.

The curly head turned slowly to face him. "If you are my enemy, Vovka, please do inform me now so that I can make other arrangements for sharing my room with someone less hostile."

Vladimir smiled and shook his head ever so slightly at this provocation. It seemed to him that Boris preferred to poke with a stick to test their potential friendship rather than offer a willing open hand. *Perhaps he is not the fool I took him for earlier*, he thought to himself. "If I were indeed your enemy, Borushka, you would be a very lucky man. You may still want to reconsider your generous offer to have me occupy so much of your precious private space."

At that, Boris stood and confronted Vladimir. He held a piece of paper in his right hand. "This 'private space,' as you call it, is all I have in the world." He waved his arms about. "You have an entire palace to call home. I do not enjoy such a luxury."

When Vladimir looked at his friend's eyes he could see they had been reddened and moist. "Has that letter you are holding upset you, Borushka?"

Boris began sobbing gently. His gaze appeared focused on Vladimir through the dribble of tears and his head tilted slightly. "Borushka. That is what my mother calls me." He sniffled.

"Yes. I remember you mentioned that this morning. Has something happened to her?" The guard examined Boris for signs of distress.

Shaking the letter in his hand ever so slightly, the chef explained, "She is sad to be living by herself now with no one to take care of. I was the youngest of her children, and the last to leave. Father has been dead for years, my brother died in Crimea, and my sisters all live with their husbands far away."

"But you write to her frequently, no?"

"Yes, but it is not the same thing as having me there to tend to." Boris wiped at his runny nose. "Without me at home, she is not sure what to do."

"Perhaps Dmitri Konstantinovich could see to it you get a leave to visit her," Vladimir suggested.

A golden eyebrow twitched at the name, "Dmitri Konstantinovich is a mean, little man who does not care for me very much right now. I seriously doubt he would grant me another favor so soon."

"*Another* favor? What favor has he already given you?"

Boris fluttered his hand, "No, I meant to say 'any favor,' not 'another favor.' I have only just arrived here."

Vladimir smiled ever so slightly again, knowing that his presence in these quarters was the favor already granted. He decided to take a chance, "I am sure your mother would enjoy hearing about your time here at the Palace." Boris nodded. "You could even tell her about the Tsar's personal bodyguard who watches over her beloved little boy."

"Yes, perhaps you are correct in that." Boris chuckled and smiled as if lost in nostalgia. "It would do much to assure her that I am safe during such violent times. I am sure that when she reads what I sent her about the explosion the other night, she will demand I return to Tula immediately." He gazed down at the paper in his hand.

"Then if you let her know how secure you are with me, it will assuage her fears, and she will not be so adamant about having you return home. That is, if you wish to remain here with me." Boris's head snapped to Vladimir. "I mean if you wish to remain at the Palace in the service of the Tsar."

"Of course, Vovka," the blond head nodded, "of course."

Vladimir took another risk and stepped toward Boris, scanning with his eyes for any sign of potential intimacy.

Boris stepped toward the guard, "That is, of course, if *you* wish to continue sharing the room with *me*." His eyes angled up as if in question.

"Of course, Borushka," the dark-haired head nodded, "of course." He braved another step closer.

The blond baker stepped quickly aside, "Thank you, Vovka. I am tired now and wish to go to sleep. It was a very busy day in the kitchen, and I must return early in the morning." He yawned and stretched. "If you wish to reconsider sharing my bed, we could make such arrangements," and he gestured toward the bedding and pillows.

Vladimir looked down, "It was very cold last night. I wish to put a blanket or two underneath me. May I use one of yours, please." Even though he chose to sleep on the hard, chilly floor, it was superior to sharing a much smaller room with a few more people.

"Of course, Vovka," Boris agreed with some hesitation, "of course." He grabbed a quilted coverlet from his bed and tossed it to the other man before climbing onto his own feather-filled mattress.

позже

Shortly before sunrise the next morning, the pastry chef roused from a stimulating dream where guards pursued him throughout the Palace. When he stepped to the cold floor, he could see the body of one of those guards entrenched in layers of blankets. Stepping carefully over the billowy bedclothes, he grabbed for his togs and opened the door to his suite as quietly as possible.

In the hallway he slipped into his chef's uniform before proceeding. As Boris entered the darkened Palace kitchen, he heard someone sobbing. This surprised him as he expected he would have been the only one there at this pre-dawn hour.

Nadezhda Ivanova stood by her table, one wizened hand to her face. She turned about at the sound of unexpected footsteps, her eyes wet and red.

Boris approached her with one hand out. "Nadezhda Ivanova, what ever is the matter?"

She wiped at her eyes and nose with one hand. "Boris Mikhailovich, I was not expecting anyone so early."

"I had planned to prepare breakfast blintzes for the Royal Family, and I needed some extra time for the yeast rising. What is wrong?"

Nadezhda sniffed and swallowed, "Ludmilla Maximova, the woman who held your post," Boris nodded, "had left because she was with child. I just received a notice that she succumbed during the childbirth." The large woman began sobbing again.

"My goodness," Boris attempted to put a comforting hand on his supervisor's shoulder, but she turned away suddenly. "Did the child survive?" Nadezhda nodded. "And what of the father?" Nadezhda shook her head back and forth a few times. "I see."

As the kitchen chief continued weeping, Boris's mind began to assemble some ideas. "Nadezhda Ivanova, what will become of the baby?"

"Such children become wards of the State and are placed in orphan homes. Not a pretty future for one so vulnerable." She coughed repeatedly.

"Are they attempting to find a home for the child?" Nadezhda continued to cough but managed to shake her head. This gave Boris his opportunity. "I might know of a place for the baby. Whom would I contact?"

Nadezhda stopped hacking and stared at Boris.

"No! Not me, my goodness." His hand went to his chest. "My mother in Tula is lonely now that I have left, and it might be a good thing for both of them. Do you not think so?"

The older woman took a few steps toward the young man, reached out both of her short arms and gave him a tight, bear hug. "Yes, let me contact the hospital where the boy is, and I will provide them with your information."

"A boy," contemplated Boris. "It is a boy." He smiled unconsciously and then spoke aloud, "I write my mother every evening, and I shall ask her opinion of this situation. If she is amenable, I will let you know as quickly as I can." He turned to his station, remembered something important, and turned back to his supervisor. "Will you—or somebody else—be able to keep the child for a few days—and as much as a week, possibly?"

Nadezhda smiled through her tears and nodded her head. It appeared Boris had inadvertently devised a way to keep two older women happy.

Boris turned back to his station but then quickly pivoted, "Oh! Please do not tell anyone of our arrangement. I do not wish others to know about this for I fear they already dislike me sufficiently." He placed a hand on his chest. "It is to be a private, family matter, if you please."

The older woman smiled, tears still moistening her leathery cheeks. "I understand your concern, but there is one person I absolutely must tell about this, Dmitri Konstantinovich."

"Dmitri Konstantinovich!?" the pastry chef sputtered. "He is absolutely the last person I wish to have know about this." His arms began gyrating through the early-morning haze. "Dmitri Konstantinovich does not like me at all! I believe he would use this against me in an attempt to remove me from this employment."

Nadezhda nodded gently. "I have heard what you say, and I agree that Dmitri Konstantinovich is probably not your closest friend in all the Palace. However, this might be information you want him to know because Ludmilla Maximova was his brother's wife."

Boris's eyes opened wide in amazement. "I see," he muttered. "Yes, if he is the last remaining family member–by all means–let Dmitri Konstantinovich know. I would certainly want to know if it were my orphaned nephew." He turned to his station to begin working on batter for the blintzes but thinking of how his mother taking the orphaned baby would help his position in the Palace kitchen as well.

After the Royal Family had finished their morning meal, and after the kitchen had been cleaned, a shiny man with a shiny head in a shiny suit appeared. Dmitri Konstantinovich turned a glassy squint toward Boris as he approached

Nadezhda. The two left the room together and did not return until Boris had put his babka for the evening meal into the oven.

The kitchen chief dabbed at her teary eyes as she walked back to her table. Dmitri Konstantinovich stared at Boris in a way that could not be interpreted easily. An involuntary shudder shook the pastry chef as he momentarily caught the gaze of his superior. The shiny, little man put an arm around Nadezhda, gave her a quick squeeze and then pirouetted on his heel striding purposefully toward the door without saying anything. As he reached for the knob, he turned his face back and commanded, "Boris Mikhailovich. A word."

Boris wiped his flour-dusted hands on a linen and approached the Chief-of-Staff. "Yes, sir?"

Before speaking, Dmitri Konstantinovich visually scrutinized the young man's face. "Nadezhda tells me you volunteered to find a home for my dead brother's baby."

"Yes," Boris spoke before realizing it might have been better to keep quiet. "I believe this might be…"

"Please!" Dmitri Konstantinovich held up a sweaty palm to silence Boris. "I will speak. You shall listen." Boris nodded. "If you think this further… volunteerism is some kind of ploy to butter my bread," he accused, droplets of sweat forming on his already moist forehead, "do not believe, for one moment, that this little stunt of yours will curry any favor with me!" and he stabbed a pudgy finger toward Boris, who stood with his jaw hanging open in disbelief.

"But… but… you don't…" the pastry chef sputtered, in a useless attempt to explain that when he made the offer, he

had no idea the orphaned baby had a connection to the distraught Chief-of-Staff.

"I do not wish to hear your illegitimate excuses!" the diminutive martinet proclaimed. "Now, back to work with you!"
He opened the door and exited quickly into the lengthening
afternoon shadows.

Boris stood gawking at the spot just vacated by Dmitri
Konstantinovich, who should have, by any account, been
thanking him for offering the Chief-of-Staff's orphaned
nephew a home. He gazed over at Nadezhda, who merely
shrugged and started to say, "No good deed…" before she
interrupted herself with paroxysms of coughing.

позже

That evening, as he sat composing a letter to his mother,
explaining the situation with the orphaned child, and inquir-
ing whether she would want to raise him, Vladimir
Yuryevich entered the room holding what appeared to be
fabric and wood. Boris looked behind him, saw Vladimir,
and asked, "What ever is that?"

The guard placed the bundle on the floor before responding,
"It is a temporary bed, you see. The floor has been rather
cold these last few nights and I have not slept well at all."
He knelt and began to assemble the cot.

"But I have invited you to share my bed with me, Vovka."
He sounded a bit pouty. "It is quite large enough for two."

A placid smile creased Vladimir's face. "Yes, I know,
Borushka, but I believe I would be uncomfortable at this
point as we still are just getting to know each other."

Boris's face flopped. "I hope that you soon feel comfortable enough to join me. It is strange having you sleep on my floor."

"If you prefer, I could return to my bunk in the barracks." He continued to work on the field bed. "As you might recall, my particular quarters were unharmed."

"No, no!" Boris stood from the desk and approached the man who had appeared in his most recent dream. "I would not hear of it." Vladimir stood, having completed the assembly, allowing Boris to examine the guard's well-fitting tunic. "Perhaps after we spend more time together tomorrow you will feel differently."

"Perhaps. Perhaps." Vladimir smiled again. "But for now, I must turn in as it is His Imperial Majesty's custom to review the troops on Sunday mornings, and I must get an early start. Good night, Borushka." He doffed his robe, which gave Boris yet another opportunity to see his friend's muscles directly.

"Good night, Vovka," he tried to say without it sounding too sentimental.

Catherine II, in an effort to further legitimize her claim upon a throne she had acquired by marriage rather than inheritance, commissioned in 1770 a bronze figure of Peter the Great, founder of St. Petersburg. Completed in 1782, it stands along the riverfront in Peter's Square, a few blocks from the Winter Palace. This imposing piece portrays a young and formidable Peter riding gallantly upon a rearing horse, one of its hind hooves crushing a snake. The statue sits upon the largest piece of solid rock ever moved by human beings. The stone weighed approximately 1,500 tons upon its discovery a few miles away, and it took almost three years to relocate to its current position. This sort of devotion to absolute sovereigns has undoubtedly waned over the centuries. The sculpture is affectionately called "The Copper Horseman."

For a Sunday morning in February, the temperature felt uncharacteristically warm. Vladimir rolled slightly before realizing he had slept in a narrow soldier's cot and there was nowhere to move. He could hear the muted snores of the blond pastry chef with the aquiline nose who slumbered upon the feather bed nearby.

The guard surmised that the kitchen helpers had Sunday morning to sleep in, and not wanting to disturb the cute, little fellow who had opened his room to the Sergeant, Vladimir crept quietly away to the barracks where he could prepare himself for the busy day ahead of him.

Once he had gotten cleaned up and presentable in his uniform for the day, he visited with Alexei Andreyevich, Lieutenant of the Guard, so that they could discuss the Tsar's troop review ritual.

"Ah, Vladimir Yuryevich! Come in, sit down," the squat man stood until the Sergeant had seated himself. "Yes, it is Sunday once more, and we know our Imperial Majesty enjoys attending the military roll call." Vladimir nodded in agreement. "Given the events of the week, I believe there should be a few changes in our usual protocol, yes?" Again, Vladimir nodded.

A knock at the doorframe drew the Lieutenant's attention as one of the fellows from the livery stable poked his head through. "Excuse me, Lieutenant, the carriage is ready."

"Thank you, Phillip." Alexei Andreyevich waved in a perfunctory manner. "Yes, that is one of the changes I wish to discuss with you, Vladimir Yuryevich. You may not be familiar with this, but years ago Napoleon the Third of France gifted a carriage to His Imperial Majesty, and it has sat in the stables, mostly untouched. I believe it was given as a token gesture following the battles in Crimea. At any rate, its construction makes it impervious to bullets, and I believe it might be prudent to utilize this little behemoth for a while until the unrest dies down."

"But it seems like the weather would suggest the open carriage for today." Vladimir stated optimistically. "I know His Imperial Majesty enjoys the fresh air."

"Normally I would agree with you, Sergeant, but we cannot be too careful with the life of our beloved Tsar." Vladimir looked down. "However, I do believe that we need to demonstrate our lack of fear, and we shall add a visit to The Copper Horseman following the troop review."

Unlike the Tsar's traditional, baroque open-air coach, the gift from Napoleon looked, colorless, boxy, and tomb-like. However, it would keep His Imperial Majesty safe as he traversed his capital city.

At the appointed time, Vladimir walked next to His Imperial Majesty, middle-aged, greying, but still looking regal in his military dress outfit. Armed soldiers stood at attention along the walkway. As they approached the coach, two military officers entered first. They assisted the Tsar up and into his seat. Vladimir climbed in last, giving the area one final review.

Once everyone had boarded, the horses drew the enclosed vehicle out the Palace gate, along the canal and over the Pevchesky bridge toward Mikhailovsky Manège, a colosseum-like, stucco-faced structure originally built as an enclosure for an elephant given to Anna, niece of Peter the Great, by Shah Nader of Persia in 1735.

People had lined up to see their great leader pass by along the traditional route. Vladimir and the other guards kept vigilant watch for possible trouble-makers.

As the Tsar's carriage entered the enclosed space of the Manège, soldiers marched up and back in square formations, columns and rows, every so often pausing, aiming their rifles and shouting, "Vzriva!" Due to a lack of ammunition, the men were not provided bullets and would merely make the sound of firing instead.

An hour later, the royal carriage proceeded back the way it came, except that when it reached the Royal Livery, instead of returning to the Palace, it continued on to Peter's Square. News of the Tsar's first public appearance since the assassination attempt had spread, and a few hundred people stood waiting to see their beloved Tsar.

Alexander II's crystal-blue eyes carefully peeked through the curtained window of the metallic grey carriage. Onlookers waved and cheered. Vladimir opened the door and stood for a moment, scrutinizing for would-be assassins amongst the throng. When a minute passed without incident, he nodded to His Imperial Majesty, who then stood in the doorway waving. His iconic mutton-chop sideburns connected by a bushy mustache bristled in the late-morning sun. The crowd cheered uproariously.

Vladimir tugged politely at the Tsar's sleeve, suggesting it might be prudent to return to the Palace. Alexander gave one last salute to his subjects and ducked back into the confines of the protective carapace on wheels, which returned uneventfully to the Palace.

A loud knocking at his door woke Boris unexpectedly. "Just a moment," he cried out, jumped off the bed, pulled his robe around him and stepped to the door, noticing the presence of the folded bed and the absence of Vladimir.

When Boris opened the door, the Palace Chief-of-Staff, stood staring up at the unshaven, young blond. "Boris Mikhailovich, you must come to the kitchen!"

The younger fellow wiped at his face with one hand and pulled his robe tighter with the other. "What is the matter, Dmitri Konstantinovich?"

With one grey eye focused on Boris, the Chief-of-Staff announced, "Your best friend—the Grand Duke—is having a reception this evening and he has requested that silly dish of yours, a dessert *crêpe*, or some such nonsense." He waved one hand in the air.

"*Soufflé à la Russe*, sir. It is made with ginger from Tula, my home —"

"I do not care if it is made with holy gold from English London, it must be prepared for His Highness and entourage." The little man's eyes shifted upward.

"Yes, sir. I shall get to it immediately." Boris began to shut the door.

"No, no!" screamed Dmitri Konstantinovich, "the Grand Duke does not need it until this evening. You may start preparations mid-afternoon." He started to walk away.

"Wait, please," Boris spouted, "I already have an engagement for this afternoon."

The Chief-of-Staff turned back, "Well, isn't that a shame." A smirk creased his otherwise tightened mouth. "You have your orders." Off he strutted back to his office.

Boris performed his morning toilet hurriedly and bolted out of his chamber and into the kitchen. "Nadezhda Ivanova! Nadezhda Ivanova!" He looked about in a panic, "I need your assistance."

The few people preparing food briefly stopped to observe their disruptive new comrade. Just as briefly they returned to their duties.

The kitchen chief approached Boris, placing a hand gently on his shoulder. "Boris Mikhailovich, it appears you are in a great deal of distress, but I must say I do not appreciate that you have come into my kitchen to share it with the rest of us." She coughed a few times.

"I am sorry, but a terrible thing has just happened, and I need your assistance, if you please."

The older woman looked up into the young man's eyes. "Yes, of course you do, but before you tell me about your problems, I would like to share with you some news upon the subject we discussed yesterday." She removed her hand and cradled it with the other to imitate rocking a baby.

Boris looked down at the arms moving from side to side and realized Nadezhda did not wish to speak openly about the orphaned child. "Oh, yes! The news! What news?" his face reddened with a grand smile.

"Everything is taken care of. You have a week or so to arrange things." Nadezhda looked up at Boris again. "Have you written to your mother?"

"Yes. She should respond in a day or two. Thank you so much, Nadezhda Ivanova." He began to reach out his arm to hug her, but she stepped back.

"No. No, hugging, please. Now, what brings such panic into your life today?"

Boris briefly looked up to the ceiling while considering how to explain his predicament. "I had previously agreed to attend a concert for a friend this afternoon, but Dmitri Konstantinovich came to me this morning to announce the Grand Duke is having an affair this evening and has requested my special *Soufflé à la Russe*." He looked down at her with tired eyes. "I do not believe I would be able to prepare my dish and attend the concert both."

Nadezhda nodded. "That sounds like a predicament indeed." She coughed again. "However, I believe I may be able to assist you."

"Really?" He perked up. "How?"

"If you prepare the batter—and I believe you are truly the only one who can prepare it." Boris nodded. "I can place it in the oven at the precise time so that it arrives for the Grand Duke as appointed. If that meets with your approval, Boris Mikhailovich."

Without nodding, Boris ran to the pantry to grab eight eggs, a large bowl and his special whisk from Paris.

The kitchen chief shook her head slowly, shrugged slightly and turned her palms up, "You are welcome."

"Thank you Nadezhda Ivanova!"

позже

Boris and Vladimir arrived back at their suite at almost the same time. They glanced at one another and smiled.

"And how was your day, Vovka?" Boris inquired as he opened the door, allowing the regal-looking guard to enter first.

"Normally I would not want to bore you with such trifle, but as you asked, I shall tell." Vladimir removed his hefty dress jacket and placed it upon the folded cot.

Boris moved to the mirror above the basin to inspect and adjust his hair. "Yes! By all means do. I wish to know what it is like to serve our Tsar so directly." He tousled the curls with damp fingers.

As he continued to remove his uniform, Vladimir narrated the events of his day up to this point, including the marching formations of the soldiers and their lack of ammunition.

"Vzriva!" Boris pointed his fingers and laughed as he repeated the sound. "That is so humorous. The guardians of our country make pretend gun sounds." He burst out in laughter again.

"Yes, but we, however, are not allowed to laugh about it," Vladimir grinned at Boris. "And your day? How have you faired?"

"Well," Boris exhaled heavily. "The Chief-of-Staff came to inform me that His Highness, the Grand Duke, will be hosting some friends this evening and that he has requested my *Soufflé à la Russe*. Normally I would be quite thrilled to prepare my dish for the Royal Family, but today that would interfere with our attendance of the concert."

"Ah, yes. What are you to do?"

Boris nodded. "Fortunately, I was able to enlist Nadezhda Ivanova to assist me. I prepared the batter and she will put it in to bake at the appropriate time."

"Nadezhda Ivanova is a good friend, indeed. I hope you are endeavoring to maintain a good relationship with her."

"Yes, I have found something that appeals to both our interests." Boris did not wish to reveal his offer to place the orphaned baby with his own mother.

Vladimir pulled on his grey tunic, and Boris donned a brown poddyovka.[3] "If you wear that," the guard commented and pointed, "people will think you an Old Believer."

Boris raised and lowered his eyebrows. "Let people believe what they wish. I care not." He raised his right arm and flapped his hand. "Besides, we need to get started if we are to arrive at the Conservatory on time. Do you have money for a donation?"

The Sergeant patted his side in response. Boris hopped to the door and opened it for Vladimir. The two walked along the marble-floored hallway and exited the building.

Cool afternoon air greeted them as they walked along the Palace embankment of the Neva River, one of the many waterways separating the various parts of St. Petersburg into districts and "sides," neighborhoods along the riversides. The wide concrete walkway separated the brown berm on the right from the expanse of green grass on the left.

One of the various Rostral columns peered down at the two as they passed. Erected during the early part of the 19th Century, the Roman-styled monuments demonstrated Russia's dominance of the waters. Up and down the column, reproductions of some of the more famous naval vessels' prows pointed out at right angles in several places between trophy plaques. Around the bottom sat four god-like figures representing the great Russian rivers: the Neva, the Volga, the Dnieper and the Volkhov. At the top, a brazier glowed brightly through the afternoon haze.

Near the landing of the first bridge crossing over to Vasileostrovsky Island stood a meat pie vendor. "Meat pies! Meat pies! Hot, fresh meat pies!" he hocked as he waved a pale lump of dough in the air.

"I believe I have forgotten to eat today, and I find myself a bit famished." Vladimir confessed. "I am going to get a meat pie." He began to approach the vendor, a middle-aged, potbellied, balding, unshaven, disreputable-looking fellow with bright eyes and bushy eyebrows.

"If I had known, I could have brought you something from the kitchen. Food fit for a king, not this… who knows what?" Boris pinched up his face.

"Oh, how bad could it be?" Vladimir responded. "How much?" he asked the vendor.

"Five kopecks. And you won't find a better meat pie in all of Petersburg!" His smiled displayed a few missing teeth. The ones that remained had yellow stains.

The guard reached into his pocket for a coin and handed it to the vendor. The fellow put the coin in his own pocket and pulled what looked like a glob of browned dough from a burlap sack. He smiled as he handed the pie to Vladimir. "Enjoy, sir," he admonished.

Boris watched with skepticism as the Sergeant put the pie up to his mouth.

"It feels neither hot nor fresh," Vladimir whispered. He took a measured bite, and when he pulled his teeth away, a strip of dark cloth waggled from his mouth. The guard yanked the bit of fabric from his teeth and waved it at the pie vendor. "What is the meaning of this?" he demanded.

The man laughed and his belly shook, "For five kopecks, what did you expect, silver brocade?" He continued to laugh as Vladimir and Boris exchanged looks.

"Sir, I am personal bodyguard to His Imperial Majesty, Alexander Nikolaevich. Either you return my coin or you give me a meat pie worthy of a Palace employee. Do you understand?"

A serious bow replaced the comical laugh, and the vendor reached into the sack once again and brought out a better-looking, better-smelling pie. "Here you go, sir. I apologize. I am sorry. I did not know who you were, your eminence."

Vladimir returned the first pie as he took the second. "Yes, this one feels much better, thank you." He glowered at the man for a second. "Come on, Borushka, I believe I have gotten what I paid for." He took a bite as he and Boris walked off. "Delicious! No better meat pie in all of St. Petersburg!" he shouted back to the vendor.

"Is it really any better?" Boris asked.

Vladimir angled his head shoulder to shoulder. "It isn't any worse." They laughed together and inadvertently looked into each other's eyes for an uncomfortable moment.

Both turned away at the same time, and they began walking along the riverbank. Vladimir took another bite of the meat pie.

"Tell me," the guard asked between chews, "how are you liking life at the Palace? I am sure we cannot compete with glorious Paris, no?"

"Well, yes," Boris began, glancing at his friend, "Paris certainly has its charms, but I spent most of my time in the restaurant kitchen." Vladimir nodded as he continued eating. "However, I have certainly found charm in St. Petersburg as well." He raised the corner of one side of his mouth.

"You know, Borushka," Vladimir finished the last bit of the pie, "you have certainly made a name for yourself at the Palace in a very short time."

Boris nodded droopily. "Yes, I know that Dmitri Konstantinovich does not like me, and I have no idea why."

The Sergeant laughed. "I meant you are well-liked, and rather quickly."

Really?" He brightened immediately.

"Yes. Your pastries disappear as soon as they hit the table. In fact, one of the Grand Dukes almost stabbed his father in the hand reaching for one of your desserts last week."

"I am very glad to hear these things, Vovka, because the way my coworkers in the kitchen grumble, I feared I was not well-liked at all."

Vladimir grinned. "Perhaps those who like you least are also the ones whose opinions matter least." They walked past shoeless men with only burlap fragments to keep their feet protected. Using crude axes and hammers, these peasant men broke rock fragments into rubble for use as roadway base.

Boris looked off across the river to the island as he considered what his friend had told him. "What about Dmitri Konstantinovich?"

"Dmitri Konstantinovich has reasons to dislike everyone he meets, but I believe his particular concerns with you are that he had no say in your employment at the Palace. He believes he should have complete control over who should serve His Imperial Majesty. If you like, I could put in a good word for you." As they now passed Peter's Square and the bronze statue of the Great Tsar across the way, the guard glanced at it, casually reminding him of the day's earlier duties with the Tsar.

"No, no!" squawked Boris, "Please, no. I do not want to give him yet another reason to single me out for his petty machinations." The pastry chef glanced over at Vladimir. "You said he had 'concerns.' What else?"

The guard's gaze fell to the walkway ahead of his boots. "Are you not aware of Dmitri Konstantinovich's... how would you say... inclination?"

"Inclination? Toward silky suits?"

Vladimir laughed again, "No, silly. Like you, he prefers men. Perhaps he feels threatened by your presence. You are able to do what he only dreams of."

"Like me, you say?" Boris squealed. "How do you mean, like me? Do you not include yourself in this category?"

The guard cleared his throat, "I suppose there are one or two men that have fascinated me." He turned one eye toward his friend and roommate.

Boris shook his blond curls and raised his face to the sky. "The day we met, you looked at me in a way most men do not." He looked directly at Vladimir. "Pardon my saying this, but I felt something beguiling with you, and I feel it every time our gazes lock. Am I wrong, Vovka?"

The two men walked without speaking until they reached the second bridge, where they turned left to head toward the

Conservatory. As they rounded the corner, Boris opened his mouth to speak but then stopped himself.

"Yes?" Vladimir prompted.

"I believe I like you, Vovka."

"I know. I like you as well."

"No," he faced the guard directly, "I *really* like you."

"Yes," Vladimir turned to Boris, "I know."

"Does that mean anything special to you?"

"Should it?"

"Vovka, stop playing games. I wish to be serious with you for a moment."

"Borushka, if you want to be serious with me, I hope that it would last more than just a moment." Vladimir produced his Mona Lisa smile. "I am sorry. I believe I know what you are attempting to ask, but please understand I might not be able to respond in a way that would be satisfactory to you. Does that make any sense?"

The slight frown on Boris's face suggested the answer. "I had hoped… Oh, never mind."

Vladimir stopped walking and faced Boris, who also stopped. "Perhaps someday I will be able to say what you want me to say and act the way you want me to act, but please understand that my current position does not allow me the kind of freedom you seem to enjoy."

Boris nodded, but just barely. "Yes, I see that. I shall endeavor not to embarrass you or have you feel uncomfortable."

"Thank you. I appreciate that, and please keep in mind that you and I are just getting to know each other now, and… well… let us just keep on getting to know each other, yes?"

They had now reached the Moyki River and began to traverse the short metal pathway of the Potseluev Bridge. The name literally means "Bridge of Kisses."

Again, Boris nodded. "Yes, you are right. I have been forward when I should just be making your acquaintance. It's just that someday I would hope to be married."

"Married? To a woman?" Vladimir opened his eyes wide.

"No, no." Boris waved his hand. "Not with a woman. With you, Vovka."

Vladimir began walking again. "Why would two sane men want to get married?"

Boris caught up. "For love, of course."

"Love?" A black cast-iron fence lined the street.

"Yes. If two people love each other, they should be able to be married."

The Sergeant huffed. "Marriage is for the merging of property ownership. Two men who already have property do not need to get married."

"But what of love?" Boris looked over with moist eyes.

"Of course they should love each other, but why bespoil that love with a marriage?"

"Are you afraid you'll end up in Kresty Prison? Male love is not illegal, you know."

Vladimir laughed. "No. I am afraid I shall end up dead."

"How do you mean?" Boris requested.

Vladimir gazed around at the precarious city encompassing him. "Much like our lovely St. Petersburg, a city always on the brink, one never knows when Vesuvius will unexpectedly rain ash and sulfur down upon it or when the ocean will suddenly rise up to reclaim its own."

"You make it sound as if Armageddon is around the corner and the Day of Judgment at hand." The pastry chef observed his new friend with unwanted suspicion.

The guard just walked on. "It is the risk we all take living in a place not originally intended for human habitation."

"And what of children?" Boris pressed. "Have you considered having children?"

The guard stopped smiling and gave the pastry chef a stern look and a nod. "I do not believe I was meant to have children." Boris shot him a surprised face. "Yes, either I am allergic to them, or they are allergic to me."

They both smiled and walked up to the entrance of the Conservatory, a squarish, brownstone building, somewhat lacking in detail. Founded in 1862 by Anton Rubenstein, most of Russia's greatest performers and composers studied under him, Zaremba, and Rimsky-Korsakov.

At the door hung a broadsheet announcing the day's charity concert, with a suggested donation of one ruble. Boris handed a coin to the young man, presumably a student, wearing a red shirt with black trim, similar to his. Vladimir fished out two ruble coins and gave them to the fellow taking the money.

"Thank you! Thank you very much, sir!" the young man blurted. Vladimir smiled in response.

As the two men entered the small, dark wood vestibule, a group of men stood talking. They wore long grey coats, long grey hair and long grey beards. Fingers pointed, punctuating well-honed bits of opinion.

"Of course Tolstoy is quite the pederast!"[4] One of the bigger, rounder fellows proclaimed. "You can observe him any Wednesday ballet at the Mariinsky Theater with the rest of the aunties. Have you not read his *Anna Karenina*? Those two soldiers. Let us agree. They were lovers, were they not?" His beady, dark brown eyes broiled the forehead of a twitchy, slender fellow with a trimmed beard who looked to the others for some assistance but got none. "Admit it, Pyotr Ilyich, we all desire the company of handsome, masculine men," and the speaker's eyes wandered to the recently-arrived Vladimir. "Well, hello there…"

One of the other tall, grey men, this one with a deeply receded hairline, stepped forward. "Ah, are you not Boris Mikhailovich, our representative from His Imperial Majesty's palace? I am glad you are here. I take it you received my missive."

"Yes. Thank you, Vladimir Vasilievich," Boris responded. "We were honored to be invited."

"I must say," the man with the receded hairline, Vladimir Stasov, continued, "I don't quite remember inviting *him*." He pointed at the Sergeant.

"Oh! Vladimir Vasilievich, may I introduce Vladimir Yuryevich, my… well… we work together."

The two Vladimirs shook hands. A few of the other men in the group looked on with eyes of curiosity and longing.

"A pleasure sir. Any friend of Boris Mikhailovich should probably be a friend of mine as well." The guard smiled with a slightly-pained look. "You seem to have caught the attention of our esteemed friend, Aleksey Nikolayevich Apukhtin. Romantic poet, staunch patriot, and poison-tongued critic, but not necessarily in that particular order." From within the hall, a bell sounded. "Shall we?"

The group entered into the concert hall, narrow but long, walnut paneling covering the walls and ceiling. Folding wooden chairs had been set up in rows. Approximately 50 people had shown up, and most had taken seats when a hushed murmur began to circulate. Faces turned toward the entrance as a stunningly-dressed, tall, slender fop with a bushy light-brown beard entered accompanied by a rather young fellow who looked quite similar to Boris but a few years younger.

"The Grand Duke!" whispered Boris.

"With someone who rather favors *you*, my friend," whispered Vladimir.

Once the two late-comers had seated themselves, Vladimir Vasilievich Stasov made his way to the front of the hall.

"My friends, thank you for joining us today to honor our greatest living Russian composer, Modest Petrovich Mussorgsky." Polite applause arose from the audience. "But before we hear from our featured performer, there are a few people who wish to share their talents with you." He stood next to the Boisselot & Fils piano and motioned to someone in the front row. "Our first piece today will be performed by our esteemed comrade, Alexander Porfiryevich Borodin."

As the audience clapped in anticipation, a rather plain-looking fellow in his late 40s stepped up as Stasov took a seat. Borodin had more the appearance of a banker or undertaker than composer and pianist. Without saying a word, he sat and began playing a contemplative, rich, harmonic piece reminiscent of a dreamy interlude on a sultry evening. Boris looked at, and scrutinized, Vladimir sitting next to him, absorbed in the melodious strains of the traditional Slavic music.

Following Borodin, the slender, nervous fellow whom the large, round Apukhtin oppressed in the antechamber stepped up to the piano. "Good evening, my friends," he said meekly, as if someone were glowering at him. "I wish to play… I shall present one movement from my piano suite, *The Seasons*. As it is now February, I feel it appropriate to play the 'Carnival' piece dedicated to this month." He began to sit but then stopped, "Oh, it is in D Major." A few people from the audience mumbled, some giggled. Tchaikovsky then played his joyous tune to everyone's delight.

Other composers and friends of Mussorgsky offered their works or those of other Russian composers. However, the highlight of the session was when Borodin, César Cui, Rimsky-Korsakov and Anatoly Lyadov stood around the piano taking turns in duets playing their humorous *Variations on the Celebrated Chop Waltz*. At its conclusion, the audience stood and applauded in amazed approbation of the amazing and entertaining performance.

Stasov returned to the front of the room. "Thank you. Thank you all. Please help yourself to refreshments at the back of the hall. In a few minutes we shall hear from the guest of honor. But first, let us please give praise to those who gave of their time to entertain us this afternoon." He indicated the assembled group of performers who stood near the piano, and the guests applauded their appreciation.

Boris and Vladimir stood. They smiled at each other. "I trust you are enjoying yourself, Vovka." The guard nodded, but then his eyes grew big and round, focused on the person behind Boris.

When he realized the Sergeant's behavior signaled the presence of someone behind him, he turned and saw the smiling, bewhiskered face of Grand Duke Alexei Alexandrovich.

"Boris Mikhailovich! Our adorable, *petit* Paris-trained pastry chef. I am glad to see you are adjusting to life in our beautiful little St. Petersburg." Dimples danced across his long face.

Boris bowed slightly and nodded. "Yes, Your Highness. Thank you once again for the opportunity to work with your family here."

The Duke laughed. "Believe me, the pleasure is ours. We all fight over your most delicious pastries, my good fellow." At his side stood a young, blond man. "I look forward to your scrumptious dessert later." He turned to the guard. "And Vladimir Yuryevich! Well… I never."

"Your Highness," and Vladimir bowed.

Without another word, the Grand Duke whisked off to the group of men in grey coats hovering around the refreshment table.

Boris and Vladimir looked at each other waiting for the other to say something. Finally, Boris could not resist, "Well, Vladimir Yuryevich… I never!" and they both burst out laughing. "Shall we get some kvass?"

As they walked toward the rear of the room, Vladimir said, "Thank you for inviting me to this concert. I am getting to see and hear people whom I have only known as names before today." Boris nodded. "This has been a very special day for me."

The bombastic Apukhtin stood near the refreshment table holding a handful of grapes he would pop into his round mouth during the rare times he stopped speaking. "Thank goodness we did not have to suffer anyone playing that cursed Glinka waltz! I fear it has become more common than 'Ochi Chyornye' or even 'God Save the Tsar.'"

"But Vladimir Vasilievich," some hapless student attempted to engage him, "is the *Valse-Fantasie* not the very embodiment of St. Petersburg itself?"

Before accidentally getting drawn into the maelstrom of engaging the critic's attention-seeking argument, Boris and Vladimir changed direction, and walked away from the food.

Ten minutes later, the crowd had seated itself again. With no introduction, Mussorgsky appeared, crumpled and disheveled. His hair looked as if it had not been combed in a week, and the whiskers on his face appeared about the same. He sat at the piano and began playing *Pictures at an Exhibition*. His fingers flew and the piano sang the sad tales of Viktor Hartmann's drawings.

In 1870, Stasov had introduced his two friends: Mussorgsky, the brooding composer, and Hartmann, the struggling architect. Over the next few years, Mussorgsky hankered and yearned over the younger, attractive but staunchly heterosexual Hartmann. In August 1873, the architect died abruptly from a ruptured artery. Ever the entrepreneur, Stasov arranged a showing of Hartmann's drawings and paintings at the Academy of Fine Arts. Moved by the experience of seeing the talents of his unrequited love, Mussorgsky composed a suite of tone poems based on a dozen of these works of art. Since its premier in 1874, *Pictures at an Exhibition* had been one of his most requested pieces.

After about 30 minutes, Mussorgsky banged out the concluding chords of "The Great Gate of Kiev." When the echoes of the final resounding bass notes faded away throughout the silent haze of the hall, the audience rose as one to applaud the performance. The composer merely sat on the bench mopping his sweaty brow, apparently unaware of the adulation bestowed upon him.

Stasov rushed up, shook Mussorgsky's arm and indicated the ovation. "Come on. Greet your patrons, Modest. Heaven knows, Jesus himself suffered more than you," the entrepreneur attempted to provide the necessary motivation. Like a sack of unruly potatoes, the composer attempted to stand, having to put one hand on the piano for leverage. Not only sweat but tears now moistened his face.

Many people in the audience began to leave, but some of the other musicians approached Mussorgsky. Boris and Vladimir stood and began walking toward the exit.

"Well, what did you think?" Boris inquired.

Vladimir pouted his lips before responding, "I am probably not the best judge of musical quality. All I ever hear anymore is military marches."

The chef laughed at the unexpected response, "No, I meant to ask if you enjoyed yourself. What of the *Pictures at an Exhibition*?"

"Oh, well, yes," the guard stumbled, "I had never heard it played before in its entirety like that. Most grand. Quite a treat to have it performed by the very composer himself."

"I am glad you enjoyed yourself. Perhaps we can attend another performance together in the future." Boris looked at his friend with hopeful eyes.

"Yes, of course, but only when my schedule permits."

"Yes, of course."

As Boris and Vladimir walked out, Rimsky-Korsakov's booming voice rang out over the din, "Modest Petrovich! You must write this piece out before it is too late! You cannot go on playing from your addled memory forever. We do not wish to lose this national treasure of yours."

"He does not look well," Vladimir commented as they reached the entry to the Conservatory.

Boris looked back at his old friend, the lively sprite whom he had first met at a Bacchanal in Paris, whose glazed eyes now suggested a broken Russian spirit and the desire for escape from the well of self-torture he had allowed himself fall into.

---

[1] 1 *arshin* = 71 cm or 2 ft. 4 in.

[2] Enacted in 1832, during the reign of Nicholas I, father of the current Tsar, Article 995 sought to outlaw homosexual acts, but courts interpreted the law to mean anal intercourse between men only. All other acts performed in private between consenting adults were not prohibited.

[3] A long, double-breasted shirt popular in Tula but also with an orthodox religious group called the Old Believers who broke with the Russian Orthodox Church in 1666 when they disagreed with liturgical reforms.

[4] The concept of homosexual or same-sex culture did not exist in Russia at that time. The term 'pederast' was used inaccurately to refer to men who preferred other men, even by these same men. It appeared to refer to the practice implemented by the Ancient Greeks.

A storybook castle—or palace—may provide shelter, but it might not provide all the comforts of a home. The Tsar's wife, Maria Alexandrovna, disliked the generally colder, damper climate of St. Petersburg and spent much of her time in warmer, drier climates. After bearing eight children, her doctors advised her to discontinue marital conjugation. In her absence, His Imperial Majesty, Alexander Nikolaevich, took several mistresses, but he favored the daughter of a minor prince, Catherine Dolgorukov, who was 30 years younger. The two met in 1864 and enjoyed a platonic friendship until the death of the Tsar's eldest son, Nicholas, the following year, when they finally consummated their relationship. At that point, Alexander told Catherine, "Now you are my secret wife. I swear that if I am ever free, I will marry you." He even appointed her as lady-in-waiting for the Tsaritsa. Maria's health declined due to "consumption" (tuberculosis), and she died in late May 1880.

In early July, Alexander married Catherine in a secret ceremony at the Alexander Palace, a royal retreat in Tsarskoe Selo, just south of the city. Not only did this action anger his family and the court, it was a direct violation of the Russian Orthodox custom of waiting at least 40 days to remarry after the death of a spouse. The Church held that the soul of the departed remains wandering the Earth during this 40-day period, returning home and visiting prior residences, as well as the fresh grave site.

His Imperial Majesty legitimized his morganatic wife by titling her Princess Yurievskaya, and she signed a proclamation renouncing any claim on the throne for herself or her children. The Royal couple requested a formal dinner to celebrate their new relationship, and both of our loyal servants continued to progress in developing their own.

Section Two:
Sour Apple Pastilas

July 1880
Winter Palace Kitchen, St. Petersburg

When Boris heard about the Royal dinner party, he knew he wanted to prepare the Tsar's favorite dessert for the occasion, a fruit pâté known as Sour Apple Pastilas. As these treats take hours to prepare, he went to the kitchen before dawn, hoping to get an early start.

Three dozen of Russia's finest sour apples had arrived the previous afternoon, and he set them in a large ceramic-coated metal colander to wash off the dust before he could begin the arduous task of peeling. Boris had not yet shaved or washed for the day because he wanted to get as much work done as possible before performing his morning ritual. With the kitchen empty and quiet at this hour, he was able to pursue his task without interruption.

His thoughts kept drifting to the boy child his mother had taken to raise. The untimely death of the woman he replaced, coincidentally the sister-in-law of the increasingly intolerable Chief-of-Staff, provided the impetus for this chapter of his life. The pastry chef's mother had eagerly agreed to take the orphaned boy, but only on the condition that she could rename him Mikhail, in honor of her late husband.

She had arrived a week later with her younger sister, Auntie Oksana, and it was good to see his mother again, as it had been over a year since he had left for Paris. At every opportunity she kissed her youngest on the cheek, which reddened further with each peck.

Boris wept with pride as he gave them a tour of his new home. When his mother met Vladimir, it was as if the two had known each other for years already, most likely due to the detailed letters sent by Boris.

Just as he began considering which schools might be best for the boy, the door to the kitchen opened, and he nicked a finger with the paring knife as he looked to see who was there. Two dark figures entered, and Boris stood to meet them. As they got closer, he could make out the diminutive form of Dmitri Konstantinovich, but the other person wore a black mantilla over her face.

"And this is the kitchen where – Boris Mikhailovich! I was not expecting to see anyone in here this early. Nevertheless, I need to speak with you–as it turns out–so it's all for the best, I suppose." The Chief-of-Staff led the visitor toward Boris. "This is Svetlana Grigoryevna, companion of Nadezhda Ivanova." His voice sounded subdued and tentative, not like his usual stentorian tone. "And this is Boris Mikhailovich, our newest addition. A pastry chef."

The woman in black held her gloved hand out to Boris, who took it lightly and kissed it before stepping back. She reached into her pocket to retrieve a handkerchief and raised it to her hidden eyes under the mantilla.

"Nadezhda is… no longer with us," the Chief-of-Staff stammered, and soft weeping could be heard from Svetlana, "and I am here to inform you that…" He paused long enough for

Boris to worry about his continued employment at the Palace. Dmitri swallowed before continuing, "… that it has been decided to promote you to kitchen chief."

"Me?" Boris reacted before thinking.

"You seem surprised, Boris Mikhailovich."

Boris nodded.

"As you are the only one who has had formal training, and–of course–your special relationship with the Grand Duke, it was an obvious choice. Besides, Nadezhda Ivanova had previously indicated to me that it was her wish for you to take her place when the time came." Dmitri smiled, but just barely.

Boris attempted to speak, but no words formed. He then realized his finger had been bleeding, and he quickly shifted it into his mouth.

"Ah, one of the hazards of kitchen service, I presume," Dmitri now spoke with his familiar, smarmy tone. "Please see me in my office at your earliest convenience. We have much to discuss." He took Svetlana's arm and the two walked off on a brief tour of the building.

Kitchen chief! Boris thought as he returned to his dessert preparations. He could not wait to write to his mother about this unexpected turn of events.

With only a few more apples to peel, the door opened again, but this time it was his friend, Vladimir Yuryevich. The apple and knife dropped into the bowl, and Boris rushed up to the guard and hugged him.

"And a good morning to you!" Vladimir did not return the hug, but merely stiffened. "What brings about this joyous greeting?"

Boris stepped back, brushed the hanging curls from his eyes and looked up at Vladimir. "I am now the kitchen chief!" He smiled as he said the words out loud for the first time.

"Kitchen chief? What about Nadezha Ivanova?"

"Oh," now he had to relate the bad news. "Dmitri Konstantinovich told me earlier this morning that she is no longer with us. Her friend, Svetlana, was with him."

Vladimir wiped at a tear. "I am saddened to hear that, but I know she had been suffering ill health for a while now. She served many years here and was always my friend. Dear woman. At least she can be at peace. I shall miss her company." He looked off into a dark corner.

"Yes. It is sad, indeed, but now I will have to be in charge here, and there is a celebration dinner to prepare." Boris studied Vladimir's far-away stare. "I hope you are happy for me."

The guard turned back, "Yes. Happy. For you. Happy. Yes. I had just come to see what got you up and out so early. What is it you are concocting?"

A skirt of apple peelings covered the work table and much of the floor around Boris. "This will be pastilas for the dinner." He pointed his arms at the bowl of peeled apples as if indicating the crown jewels.

"Ah! His Imperial Majesty is quite fond of pastilas. I am sure he will be suitably impressed." Vladimir nodded as he gazed upon the pulpy, white orbs. Then he looked at the face of his roommate. "But not so impressed with your appearance, I fear." He wiped at his own clean-shaven cheeks. "It seems you have some personal duties to attend to as well."

"Yes," Boris agreed penitently. "I was in such a hurry this morning to begin the dinner obligations that I neglected my own."

"Well, I must be off. I have my own obligations awaiting me, given that we are to prepare the rest of the staff for your most excellent meal." He strutted to the door. "Until later, my friend, and–under the circumstances–congratulations."

"Yes, later. Thank you!" Boris returned to his peeling, speculating what Dmitri might say to him, and careful not to cut another finger.

Once the apples had all been peeled and cut, Boris set them to soak in the honey-sweetened solution before they would be ready for boiling. During this time he could visit with the Chief-of-Staff to find out what things needed discussion.

When he arrived at the Chief-of-Staff's office, the door stood ajar, and Dmitri sat at his desk. Boris knocked lightly.

"Come in, come in, and please close the door." The diminutive fellow stood as Boris entered and indicated a chair next to the desk. Dmitri Konstantinovich studied the other man with slightly-squinted eyes for a few seconds before speaking again. "This is a sad time, indeed." Boris looked at his superior with raised eyebrows. "Our beloved Nadezhda Ivanova is gone, my sister-in-law is gone, the Tsaritsa is gone." He paused and peered upward. "A sad time indeed." He returned his scrutinizing stare to Boris. "However, we have much work to do, and I must now instruct you regarding the expectations of your new position here."

Boris shifted in the chair, not because it was uncomfortable.

"But before we discuss Palace business, I wish to inquire into the status of my nephew… Mikhail is it?" Boris nodded. "Yes, Mikhail. And your mother has received him well?" Another nod. "It is woeful that he is almost a thousand versta[5] away, but at least I know he will be well cared for. Please tell me again why your mother agreed to raise the child of another."

Before speaking, Boris cleared his throat. "Sir, thank you for this opportunity to serve our beloved Tsar. I want you to know that I will give my best efforts for —"

Dmitri held up a palm to halt the unasked-for soliloquy. He then motioned with his hand in a circular pattern to encourage a hastier reply to his question.

"My mother was all alone and I asked if she would welcome the baby into her home," Boris continued. "This gives her a purpose again after her husband—my father—had died and her children have left the area."

Dmitri nodded, "Yes, I see. Do you write your mother regularly?"

"Every evening, sir. It is my custom."

"Then please add my well wishes the next time you correspond, and–if you can–ask her to provide updates from time-to-time so that I may have some news of my nephew."

"I will, sir." Boris reminded himself it might be best to keep his responses minimal when dealing with Dmitri.

"Thank you," Dmitri almost smiled. "Now, on to our current situation. You are to become regular Palace staff, and with that advancement comes a few rewards and a few responsibilities." He glanced at Boris, whose attention focused on him. "First, you must sign an oath of loyalty to His Imperial Majesty and the House of Romanov." He produced a printed sheet of official-looking paper.

Boris took the form, examined it briefly, picked up the pen on the desk, dipped it, and signed. "Absolutely! You will find no one more loyal, sir." He handed the paper to Dmitri.

"Yes, good. Now, I need to –"

"Absolutely! No one."

Dmitri appeared a bit ruffled at the interruption as he placed the signed form on the desk. "And you shall enter the Table of Ranks at the Palace service, a distinguished and enviable position with suitable monetary compensation."

"Ranks, sir? Like the military?"

Again, a bit of feathers bristled, "Rankings, yes, but not military. Our Ranks are numbered sequentially from the lowest dust-maid apprentice or stable cleaner at Rank One all the way up to Rank Twelve."

"And what is your rank, if I may ask. I imagine the Chief-of-Staff is close to the top, no doubt." Boris neglected to keep his interactions to a minimum.

Dmitri closed his eyes and took a breath. "No, the top ranks are for those who serve the Romanovs very closely. I, myself, am but a Rank Six." He looked down.

"I see," Boris retorted. "And what does that make me? As kitchen chief?"

"Do not press your new position with me, Boris Mihkailovich!" He stood, nostrils flaring, face inflaming. "Just because you appear out of nowhere and worm your way into the favor of the Royal Family with your cooking legerdemain does not mean you can lord your particular connections over me. Is that clear?" His reddened eyes bulged.

"I did not mean –"

"I do not care what you did not mean!" Dmitri cut off Boris. "As long as I am the Chief-of-Staff in this Palace, I shall be your superior, and you will demonstrate the proper level of respect and deference! Do you hear me?"

Boris nodded his assent.

"Good." Dmitri sat again, the violent wave passing and the color in his face receding. "Now, I need to show you the table settings for this evening so that you can plan the meal accordingly. However, you are in no condition to enter the hall in your current state. Find a suitable coat and pants, not that silly *poddyovka* I have seen you wear. A fine, European-style coat with real men's pants."

"Yes, sir." He began to stand.

"And shave yourself! Look presentable! What if a member of the Family should enter the Hall while we are there? We do not want them thinking the Palace staff is culled from the serfs trawling along the Embankment."

"Yes, sir." Boris walked to the door.

"Four!" Dmitri shouted.

"Pardon?"

"Four," he repeated. "You shall begin at Rank Four."

"Yes, sir." Boris opened the door, left the office and walked back to his suite.

Once he returned to his room, the new kitchen chief began preparing for his interview with the Chief-of-Staff regarding this evening's gala. He grabbed the soap at the wash basin and began making the lather for shaving.

His thoughts wandered to the new responsibility bestowed upon him. *Kitchen chief!* He could still not quite grasp the idea that he was now in charge of the Palace kitchen. It was the logical choice, after all. He had the proper training, thanks to Adolphe Dugléré. Nadezha Ivanova had even named him as her successor. Boris had not realized that placing his predecessor's baby meant so much to her. His mother would be so proud. Of course, the position meant much more work and less free time, but this was the profession of choice for Boris, and he intended to make as much of the situation as he could. Unfortunately, it also meant more dealings with Dmitri Konstantinovich, whose dislike of Boris was patently obvious. In addition, people would probably gossip about Boris knowing the Grand Duke, or how other deserving people got passed over, but such small minds frequently eschew reality in that sort of backside chinwag talk.

Once he finished applying the foam to his bristly face, he picked up the razor blade and studied himself in the mirror. *Where to begin?* He held the handle in his right hand while he moved his nose out of the way with his left. As he started to make his first few hasty strokes, the door opened.

Vladimir walked in and closed the door behind him. He tilted his head back slightly as he observed Boris making short, rapid motions with the razor. "Stop! Stop!" he cried, "I cannot stand to watch you do that any longer."

"Do what?" Boris paused and glanced at Vladimir. "I must get ready to meet Dmitri Konstantinovich in the banquet hall. We have much to discuss for tonight's affair."

"Please, let *me* shave you, Borushka," the Sergeant entreated.

Boris cocked his head, inadvertently slathering foam on his shirt. "Does my shaving offend you, Vovka?"

Vladimir looked up at the ceiling. "It does not *offend* me, but I keep worrying that you are going to injure yourself chop-chop-chopping like that." He demonstrated with one hand and then pointed a finger. "You shave like the French!"

Boris smiled at the accusation, rumpling the lather on his face. "Well, consider that I have spent the last few years of my life in Paris. It makes sense, yes?"

The guard covered his eyes with a hand, "I am concerned you will cut yourself or–even worse–accidentally hack something off." Boris laughed. "No, honestly, Borushka. Your methods are unsafe, unsanitary and unhealthy."

"I shave quickly. Who has time for such amenities? My 'methods'–as you call them–are efficient and modern." He brandished the razor with a flourish and foam flew off at differing angles.

Vladimir turned his cool, blue eyes upon Boris, "Would you please allow me to demonstrate on you?" The chef's eyebrows raised. "I have become accustomed to your appearance, and I would prefer you not to have bits of your face unintentionally ending up in the basin."

"And your 'methods' would be safer than mine?"

"Safe? Of course. Who do you think shaves our Imperial Majesty?" Vladimir tapped his chest with a thumb. "You will be in the best of hands. Please, allow me…"

The guard stepped up to Boris and gently took the razor by the handle. Boris stared at Vladimir and the tool in his hand. The Sergeant ran his other thumb over the naked steel to assess its sharpness.

"This blade is dull!" He proclaimed. "Where is your strop?"

Boris opened a drawer of the vanity and produced a honing stone. "This is what we use in the kitchen to sharpen our tools." He handed it to Vladimir, who examined it with a bit of a raised eyebrow.

"I see." He began to run the blade across the stone in the same manner as if he were using a leather strop.

"No, no!" protested Boris. "Let me demonstrate." He cupped Vladimir's left hand with his own as they held the stone together. Then he retrieved the razor with his other hand and began sliding it smoothly across the rough surface, drawing the entire length of the sharp edge across the top face.

Vladimir observed the procedure without commenting. After three passes along the stone, Boris handed the blade back. The guard returned the stone to Boris and then ran his thumb across the newly-honed edge.

"That's much better! Now, stand still."

As Vladimir began slowly and deliberately gliding the razor through the lather, Boris watched in the mirror, to observe this new technique. The velvety movement did not scratch or nick. At one point Vladimir glanced into the mirror as well, and their eyes caught in the reflection for one evanescent moment. Just as quickly, the Sergeant returned his attention to his duty, grooming his friend.

With each succeeding measured swipe of the blade, Boris imagined its smooth caress as kisses, and he closed his eyes in childlike reverie, smiling.

Vladimir continued to scrape the stubble from the cheeks and neck, careful to preserve that pointy goatee Boris was so proud of. The Sergeant did not seem to notice the look of ecstasy on the chef's face.

The minutes passed in relative silence, the only sounds being that of the razor on skin and tapping on the wash basin. Once Vladimir finished removing most of the soap, he looked at Boris, who stood with his eyes closed and smiling as if he were awaiting a stolen kiss. The guard-cum-barber smiled in response.

"Finished," Vladimir announced as he reached for the hand towel nearby. Boris opened his eyes and observed his reflection in the mirror. "Here," the guard passed the cloth and began dunking the razor in the basin.

Once he wiped off the excess lather with the towel, Boris ran his free hand over his cheeks and neck. "Very nice. Very nice, indeed." He nodded.

"You're welcome," came the curt response. "Now you look mostly presentable."

"*Mostly* presentable?" Boris squawked. "What exactly do you mean, Sergeant?"

Vladimir turned his attention to the chef's comfortable clothes that might be suitable for kitchen work, but not for going into the rooms of the Palace.

Boris looked down at his outfit. "Oh, yes. I need to obtain a man's suit. Do you know where I can get one in a hurry?"

The guard placed the clean razor on the vanity top. "If you wish, I will visit with the royal tailor while you continue your toilet. I am certain we can find something for you."

"At the royal tailor?"

"Yes, we were at the Academy together, and I am sure he will provide something… suitable." Vladimir smiled at his little jest.

"Yes. Thank you, Vovka. Please." Boris returned to the basin as Vladimir left the chamber.

A blond, curly head stared back from the mirror. He had just been shaven by the man he felt closest to, an emotionally intimate experience unlike any before, including his nighttime trysts at the Turkish Baths. This Vladimir awakened feelings Boris had never expected. It had been difficult enough with the gorgeous guard sleeping on the floor of his suite every night. Now, after this incredibly close encounter, he did not know how he would be able to conduct himself. He could only hope that his choice of companion would choose him in return.

As he continued to stare at his own image, the door opened again and Vladimir reappeared. In one hand he held some clothing. Boris's head snapped toward the door.

"Borushka, it's not much, but it's all I could find. The tailor had very little left because of the gala this evening. I hope this fits you." Vladimir handed the silken suit coat and woolen pants to Boris, who placed them on the bed.

Boris picked up just the wool pants, dyed jet black and somewhat heavier than he was used to. He held them up, giving an eyeball measurement. "They appear somewhat large, but I shall give them a try." He bent over and pulled the trousers up as far as they would go. The cuff rested gently on the floor, but the waist reached up to his bottom rib and appeared to have been made for someone with much more girth. Boris looked at Vladimir with one eyebrow raised.

"Do you not have a belt?" Vladimir suggested.

Boris picked up his *poddyovka* with one hand, having to hold the oversized pants with the other. He managed to wrestle the knitted, scarf-like belt and drop the shirt to the floor. Even after wrapping it around himself twice, the hanging ends dangled to his knees. Boris looked at Vladimir with the one eye again.

"Try on the coat."

The silver-grey silk shimmered even in the dappled light of their room. A thin, black lapel graced the neckline, giving it an air of sophistication. His arms glided into the sleeves and, while they were just a bit too long, the jacket fit his chest quite well. He glanced at Vladimir, but this time with a smile.

"You look very dashing, Borushka." And he returned the smile.

Boris stepped toward the mirror so that he could see himself in these new clothes. The belt from the *poddyovka* still showed from beneath the jacket, and he worked the loose ends into the waist so that they were no longer visible. When he looked again, he saw the Tsar's new kitchen chief, Service Table Rank Four, Boris Mikhailovich Zelany.

"Thank you, Vovka. It is just what I needed. I can only hope Dmitri Konstantinovich approves."

Vladimir's eyes took in the new wrappings. "I am certain he will approve."

"I certainly hope so." He sat to put on his shoes. "He is probably waiting for me in the banquet hall now."

"Yes, you should hurry. We shall speak later."

Boris turned to face Vladimir directly. His eyes wandered over the fetching guard's muscular body. How remarkable that a poor boy from Tula could rise to the level of kitchen chief to the Tsar and have a close companion as delightful as Vladimir. The feelings of gratitude overwhelmed him, and he stepped forward, reached out and hugged his friend tightly.

"Thank you again." Boris whispered into Vladimir's ear, then he dropped his arms and fled out the door.

His shoes clacked rhythmically as he ran across the marble-tiled floors and colonnaded limestone courtyard. He jogged through the passageway to the Parade Halls and crossed to the Great Hall, where the banquet would be that night. Boris had never been in this section of the Palace before, and at first viewing, it overwhelmed him.

Every wall had enormous paintings covering them. Family portraits, landscapes and military officers in celebrated battle scenes sneered down at him. The checkerboard pattern on the floor caused a bit of disorientation as well. When he stepped into the hall itself, his field of vision filled with the largest chandelier he had ever seen. Thousands of sparkling strings of crystals ringed with gold dangled precariously above. Smaller versions hovered throughout the grand room. Beneath them, the banquet tables had been arranged in the shape of a large letter 'A' (presumably for Alexander), with the apex pointing toward the doors to the Court Garden beyond. Intricate lace cloths covered the tables and almost a hundred place settings awaited their meal to come.

"I am so glad you could make it in due course before the food arrived," snarked Dmitri as he stepped from behind a dark green marble column.

"I'm sorry, sir," Boris responded, bowing slightly. "I needed to prepare myself and obtain the suit you requested."

Dmitri appraised the borrowed clothing with one eyebrow raised, "Well, it will have to do for this evening because you had such short notice, but please assure me that first thing tomorrow you will obtain some proper menswear. If you are to continue in this position, you shall require appropriate clothing when traipsing through these rooms of State." He fluttered a gloved hand to indicate the hallowed hall.

"Yes, of course, sir. Straightaway." Boris gawked at the furnishings of the room. More daunting paintings hung from the walls and over the fireplaces. The gold leaf of the frames glinted in the bits of sunlight that filtered through the gauzy curtains.

"Over here, please." Dmitri had moved to one of the place settings.

Boris approached the table and his jaw fell open. Amongst a parade of polished silver candelabra, the dizzying array of glasses, platters and gold-plated tableware mesmerized him. To the left of a service plate sat four forks of various sizes. To the right, four different knives plus a soup spoon with an oyster fork resting in its bowl at an oblique angle. Upon the platter sat an ornate silver napkin holder with a rolled-up red cloth and a place card, the name written in gold ink. Beyond this were various stemmed glasses, a salt cellar, a nut dish, more forks and spoons, a salad plate, and a butter knife leaning upon a cut crystal rest.

"Unlike your *service à la française*," the Chief-of-Staff intoned, "where you merely toss all of the food upon the table at once and the guests have a whimsical free-for-all," he rolled his eyes, "here we provide *service à la russe*, where each course is served sequentially, and each guest receives their own separate portion, thereby assuring the proper temperature of the food." He nodded and smiled as if he had invented the whole concept himself.

Boris continued to take in the dazzling array set out before him. Dmitri waited a few seconds before continuing.

"Fortunately for you, Nadezhda Ivanova had already planned the meal, and you have but to execute it according to her design." He pulled a crumpled piece of paper from an inside pocket and handed it to Boris. The blocky scribbles displayed a lack of formal education by their writer. "As you might have discerned, the diners begin with the outermost tableware and work their way to the center as the meal progresses." Dmitri pointed to one of the oyster forks, diagonally poised as if laughing at the other utensils. "This is used for either oysters or caviar, and as oysters are out of season due to the warm weather, we shall be enjoying our favorite Malossol this evening."

On the scrawled list, Boris found the lightly-salted caviar at the top. He had never tasted such a delicacy before, but he should try it before serving, if only to make sure it would be fit for the Tsar's party.

"The beverages," and Dmitri indicated the copse of stemware, "are handled by the table servers, so you need not worry yourself with that." The Chief-of-Staff's slightly raised chin indicated his sense of superiority over the new kitchen chief, even though he stood a few *dyuim*[6] shorter. "It shall be mostly Kvass with assorted wines and fortified beverages." Boris nodded out of habit. "Do you have any questions before you return to your kitchen?"

Nadezha's list contained so many items, but none totally unfamiliar. "I believe I can deliver the meal as requested, sir." Boris smiled at his superior not because he was happy but because he knew he could fulfill his new position quite well, and that would remove any grounds for potential disciplinary action. Even as he reviewed the proposed meal in his mind, he was already considering substitutions for a few of the dishes that had been served so commonly in the past. He wanted to make his presence known at the Tsar's table for something other than just tasty desserts.

"As you well know, the banquet begins at 18:30." The Chief-of-Staff checked his pocket watch unnecessarily. "And—by the way—I do not want to see you in this room for the rest of the day. It will be only for the house staff, not lowly kitchen help." Dmitri pivoted on his pointy toes and marched off to annoy some other member of the Palace service. Boris walked briskly back to the kitchen to arrange the meal.

The other workers busied themselves with preparing the day's food. List in hand, Boris addressed his former peers for the first time as their chief. "As you all probably know by now, Nadezhda Ivanova is no more." A few of the women raised a sleeve to their eye. Most of the kitchen workers had known her all their lives. "And you have most likely heard that I have been chosen as her successor." A few coughs punctuated the brief silence. "I am sorry, but we will have to postpone our mourning for a while because today we are charged with preparing a sumptuous feast for our beloved Tsar and his new wife." He had chosen his words carefully because not everyone accepted his bride as legitimate. "Please listen carefully as I read off the menu."

During the next 15 minutes, Boris discussed the dishes and who would be responsible for their preparation. Following the Malossol caviar would be cheese and egg in molded aspic, borscht for the soup, salmon steak as a first main course, wildberry sorbet, garden greens in vinaigrette, game hens in lemon and pepper for the second main course, and, lastly, his special Sour Apple Pastilas for dessert. Fortunately, Nadezhda had stocked the hens previously that week, and the wildberry sorbet had been delivered that morning. Boris substituted the fresh green salad for a sliced fennel dish that had seen too many evenings at the Tsar's table. He hoped this new course would earn him some praise.

The new kitchen chief thought there might have been some dissension because of his elevation over the others, but only once or twice did he observe an indignant eye. After he finished delegating the work, he returned to his apples and prepared them for boiling.

Chef de cuisine, he thought to himself, *yes, that should be my proper title. Many of the household staff have French designations, and my position should reflect that fashion.*

When the boiled apples reached a thick, gooey consistency, Boris poured the mixture into baking pans and leveled them off with a long, flat blade. The pastilas would then have to cook in the oven until they were no longer sticky.

As his special dessert baked, Boris wandered about the room, observing the others, being careful not to speak unless spoken to. He did not want to begin his reign as *chef de cuisine* on the wrong *pied.* Everyone seemed to be quite comfortable with the new arrangement. Perhaps no one wanted the responsibilities, the extra hours, or the stress of having to deal more directly with the rather disagreeable Chief-of-Staff.

At half past six, Dmitri appeared in one of his shiny, silken suits. He looked around the room for the newly-appointed kitchen chief but did not see him. "Boris Mikahilovich!"

Boris stepped from the larder with the greens for the salad in a large wooden tub. "Yes, sir?"

"The Tsar and his bride have arrived in the banquet hall. Serving staff should be coming in at any moment. Is everything ready?"

Boris smiled proudly. He glanced around the room, stopping to make eye contact with each of his staff. "Thank you all. You have done very well, indeed." He then turned to Dmitri, "Yes, sir. All is prepared." He bowed unnecessarily.

With a sly smile, the Chief-of-staff left the kitchen and walked back to the hall where the banquet would soon begin.

позже

After the last platter of pastilas had been sent to the table, Boris inspected each of the working stations to make sure that they had been properly cleaned. He dismissed the staff, thanking them again for all their hard work. As they began to file out, Dmitri Konstantinovich pushed his way in. His sweat-drenched bald pate glimmered in the evening light.

"Boris Mikahilovich!" came the shout. With bulging eyes that darted about, his head swiveled left and right. The remaining kitchen staff scurried past to get to the exit.

A head of blond curls turned around. "Yes, sir?" He still wore the silver-grey suit with the thin, black lapel Vladimir had obtained for him earlier in the day.

The Chief-of-Staff's gaze focused upon Boris and he waited until all the others had left. "There was an unauthorized substitution on the menu that Nadezhda Ivanova had prepared," he growled through gritted teeth.

"Yes, sir. Was that a problem?"

Dmitri stared at the new kitchen chief in disbelief and slowly shook his head back and forth. "There was supposed to be a fennel dish before the second main course. Instead, the guests received greasy weeds from the garden." His lips and nose combined in a sneer. "How did that happen, kitchen chief?"

Boris raised himself up as tall as possible. "If you please, sir, I would prefer to be called '*chef de cuisine*' as it —"

"*Chef de* **what**?" Dmitri squawked. "This is a Russian household, and our servants shall have Russian titles."

"Yes, sir. Many do, but I would like use this title because it more closely represents my station."

"You can call yourself whatever you want, but as far as I am concerned, you are my kitchen chief, and that's that. Do I make myself clear?" The Chief-of-Staff's eyes burned like hot coals.

"Yes, sir. As you wish," Boris demurred.

"And what happened to the fennel?"

"Oh, we were out of fennel and I thought I would attempt a new dish, one incorporating vegetables from the garden. Did the guests dislike my salad? If so, I shall never serve it again."

Dmitri stared at Boris with tightly balled fists as if he had difficulty assembling his thoughts. After an uneasy pause, he relaxed his grip and inhaled audibly. "As it turns out, Princess Catherine, the new wife of His Imperial Majesty, spoke quite favorably about it. She stated she missed having fresh greens and she hoped this dish would appear more frequently at the table."

Boris smiled to himself as minimally as possible in hopes that his superior would not observe his self-satisfaction.

"In the future," Dmitri continued, "see to it that all changes of order are approved by me first. Do you understand?" Boris nodded silently. "As an added incentive, I am suspending your pay for one week."

"But sir –" Boris attempted to object.

The Chief-of-Staff cut him off with the sharp wave of a hand, "Unless you would like me to make it two weeks," he held up two fingers with a snarl.

"No, sir." The kitchen chief's face pointed toward the floor.

"Good." Dmitri turned toward the door and then turned back. "And see to it that the new Princess has her dish as requested."

"Yes, sir," Boris acknowledged, half joyful that his creative choice pleased the new Royal family member but half sad that his rash action caused him to lose a week's pay.

Once he finished his final walkthrough of the kitchen, he returned to his suite, hoping to find Vladimir so that he could tell his friend about this glorious day and its peculiar ending. Unfortunately, Vladimir's duty required him to stand at the Tsar's side, and the Sergeant would not be returning to their room for quite a while.

Boris took off the suit and pants, removing the oversized waistband and returned it to his *paddyovka*. Despite the evening hours, a slurry sun still hovered well above the horizon at this time of year. He sat at his desk and wrote to his mother, informing her of his unexpected promotion and making sure to include Dmitri's request for updates on his nephew.

Once he finished the letter, he donned the long brown shirt, tied its waistband around him and walked outside. The air felt cool on his still-smooth face, and an hour or so of daylight remained. He started off toward Nevsky Prospekt hoping to enjoy the social atmosphere of one of the last White Nights[7] before the season changed.

Off to the left in the harbor, he could see ships with different solid-color sails drifting along. In celebration of the lengthy hours of sunlight during the mid-year, boat captains furled the usual, pale canvas sails and hoisted brightly-hued ones instead, giving the waterfront the sensation of a rippling rainbow.

As he rounded the corner onto the wide boulevard, music surged from buildings all around him. Opera, folk songs, popular ballads of the day. A most joyous celebration of the summertime late evening.

People, mostly in couples, strolled by. Some of the café patrons spilled out onto the sidewalks. Pale orange rays of light bathed the scene in a creamy sorbet. Even with all this humanity about him, Boris felt like something was missing, but he wasn't quite sure of what it might be. He had been elevated to *chef de cuisine*, something to be quite satisfied with, and yet that was not enough. He had overseen the preparation of an eight-course feast for His Imperial Highness with very short notice, another amazing accomplishment. What could it have been? What emptiness still consumed him?

At the *Passage*, where he had hoped to meet other fellows interested in meeting other fellows, the ambience felt peculiar and awkward. More like one of those French Impressionist's paintings, billowy and out-of-focus. Men followed him with their eyes as he walked by, smiling, nodding. Again, something he would have generally enjoyed, but tonight was different somehow, and he just kept walking.

The sun's disc had just touched the distant horizon and the glow of another White Night began to fade. Drawn-out shadows consumed the street in an eerie chiaroscuro of dark and dusk.

Without realizing where he had ended up, Boris found himself standing at the door of the Znamensky Baths. He then realized what it was he lacked.

He understood this might be the last time he could patronize the establishment because from that time forward, he ranked among the Palace service staff and it would be improper for him to frequent such a notorious institution. After

a bracing breath, he walked in, approached Gavrilo, the proprietor, and requested "Igor."

позже

In the morning Boris woke to the stare of two Arctic-blue
eyes from below.

"Good morning, Borushka. You came in quite late last evening. I hope you enjoyed yourself." Vladimir readjusted
himself so that he sat cross-legged on the pile of blankets. He
had stopped using the cot as it had tipped too easily, spilling
him over unexpectedly onto the floor in the night.

Boris sat up and swiveled his fists in his eye sockets to remove the crusty residue and then blinked a few times. He
did not wish to tell Vladimir what had actually transpired
for fear of him not wanting to continue developing their relationship, whatever his perception of it might be. The more
staid palace guard might not understand or approve of these
bathhouse escapades.

"Following the banquet, I took a stroll along Nevsky
Prospekt to enjoy the White Night. Thank you for asking. It
was quite celebratory."

Vladimir cocked his head. "Did you make it as far as the
Passage?"

Boris tilted his head and looked up as if trying to recall, "As
a matter of fact, I did."

"And were there men to your liking at the *Passage?*"

It started to feel like an inquisition. "There were men—to be
sure—and some of them even favored me with their glances,

but I had no interest in *them*, Vovka." Boris smiled at Vladimir.

"I see." The guard averted his gaze. "You should not be frequenting such a place now that you have a service rank, Borushka." He faced his friend again, "We must uphold a certain respectability."

Boris coughed into his fist a few times. "Yes, I understand, but I do have needs, Vovka." He stared back. "I have needs."

The two maintained eye contact for a few intense seconds.

"And how was your evening?" Boris broke the silence.

The guard began relating some of the events from the banquet, including descriptions of some of the exquisitely fashionable outfits. He mentioned that at one point, His Imperial Majesty stood in conversation with Tsesarevich[8] Alexander Alexandrovich and his brothers.

"Your superior, Dmitri Konstantinovich, entered the Hall," Vladimir narrated. "He appeared to be surveying the room for any detail that might have been neglected or omitted. His attention immediately snapped to the head of a man in conversation with your friend Grand Duke Sergei Alexandrovich," Boris pulled a pinched face, "whom he could only see from behind. The fellow had blond, curly hair–similar to yours–and he wore a silver-grey suit coat with a thin, black lapel, just like the one I obtained for you from the royal tailor."

Boris leaned closer. "I see."

"Yes," Vladimir continued, "Dmitri strutted up and shouted, 'I believe I told you I did not want to see you in this room again for the rest of the day!' and then something like, 'If you continue to disobey direct orders from your superiors, I shall have you shipped back to Paris, where you belong!' He then grabbed the man with the silver-grey suit by the shoulder and spun him around."

"Oh, my!" Boris put his hand to his mouth.

"Well, just you wait." Vladimir smirked. "'Dmitri Konstantinovich, unhand my guest immediately!' the Grand Duke commanded. He turned to the young man who was obviously not you after all, 'Nikita Iosifovich, are you unharmed?' Then he turned back to Dmitri Konstantinovich, 'Explain yourself, Chief-of-Staff.'"

Boris put the other hand up to his mouth as well and his eyes opened fully.

"Dmitri Konstantinovich suddenly pulled back his hand and capitulated, 'Your Highness,' he gasped, 'I mistook the gentleman for someone else who has the same suit of clothing. I am truly sorry and apologize for any insult I may have caused,' and he bowed deeply. Grand Duke Sergei raised his chin sharply, took his companion by the arm and they promenaded out through the Portrait Gallery to the garden."

"The other fellow must have gotten a similar suit at the royal tailor," Boris deduced. "It has been said that we have similar features."

Vladimir re-examined his roommate's face. "Yes, now that you mention it, I can see the similarity." He smiled. "Perhaps that is why the Grand Duke favors you so."

"Yes, perhaps," Boris replied. "Certainly enough likeness to confuse our Dmitri Konstantinovich." Vladimir nodded.

"That certainly explains his behavior in my kitchen last evening."

"*Your* kitchen, is it now?" Vladimir teased.

"I think you know what I mean," Boris burbled. "He ran in as I was dismissing the staff and proceeded to roast my soul for an unauthorized dish substitution."

"If memory serves correctly," the guard put a finger to his chin and glanced upward, "the last person to commit such a treasonous act is still rotting in the Lithuanian Castle."[9]

Boris frowned, "Not funny, Vovka. That *mudak* docked my pay for a week because of it. At least now I know why he was so upset."

Vladimir took a step toward his friend, "I apologize, Borushka. I did not realize. If you need monetary assistance —"

"Thank you, but no. My dear mother trained me well in the ways of frugality."

"And—it probably goes without saying—your Sour Apple Pastilas were the crowning glory of an amazing meal."

Boris stood and bowed in mock deference. "Your servant, sir." He grabbed his dressing robe and pulled it around him. "I imagine you have your usual Sunday duties with His Imperial Majesty."

"Yes, off to the parade grounds." He rolled his eyes upward. "March, march, march."

Boris laughed. "And what is that sound they make?"

"Vzriva!" Vladimir held up his arms as if shooting a rifle. "Vzriva! Vzriva! Vzriva!" he spat as he rotated back and forth in mock firing.

They both laughed heartily and lock gazes again. This time smiles replaced the stern looks.

"And you, Borushka?" Vladimir broke the stare, "What trouble will you be getting yourself into today, if I may inquire?"

"Well, since you asked, I am planning to return to the Conservatory of Music this afternoon. Madame Nadezhda Filaretovna von Meck, who is some wealthy widow and a patron of Pyotr Ilyich, discovered this French prodigy in Paris, whom she has since hired as tutor for her daughters. He is to perform later today."

"Ah, a recital. Were you planning to invite me?" Vladimir glared.

"Oh… well… I know that on a Sunday you have your regular obligations with His Imperial Majesty," Boris muddled.

"Yes, you are correct, my friend," he grinned. "However, as of late, His Imperial Majesty grows weary following this ritual, and he prefers to occupy his afternoons privately with his new bride." He glanced away. "My services are generally not required."

"I see, Vovka. By all means, please come along and rescue me from the infernal ramblings of that interminable, self-appointed Apukhtin. Perhaps we can stop along the way for a meat pie. One made with real silver brocade!" He laughed and Vladimir joined in.

Abrupt and loud knocking at their door halted the mirth. "Boris Mikhailovich!" The slightly-muffled voice belonged to Dmitri.

Vladimir stood and pushed the pile of blankets to one side. He grabbed his gown and went to the door.

"Yes, what is it, Chief-of-Staff?" the tall guard lorded over the shorter fellow, glowering down at the shiny, bald pate as he opened the door.

Without waiting for an invitation, Dmitri pushed his way into the suite and swivelled his head about, his bulging eyes surveying each wall and piece of furnishing. "Ah, Vladimir Yuryevich, it is good you are here as well because you would have heard this news soon enough."

"What news, sir?" Boris asked as Vladimir closed the door.

Dmitri stood flanked by the two taller men, and he had to bend his neck back a bit to face them. He cleared his throat. "Count Loris-Melikov[10] has commanded that he and the Tsar's party shall spend several days at Alexander Palace. Your presence has been requested, and you shall accompany the Royal party accordingly."

Boris smiled at Vladimir. "Of course, sir."

"Excuse me, Dmitri Konstantinovich," Vladimir interposed, "can you tell me why the Count has chosen to remove His Imperial Majesty from the security of this Palace and transport his party out to Tsarskoe Selo?"

With a brief shudder of his head, the Chief-of-Staff responded, "Not that you need to know this—*Sergeant*—however, it is Count Loris-Melikov's desire to further the discussion with His Imperial Majesty regarding his recommended economic and administrative reforms, and he felt the… disquiet of the city might be too distracting. In case you have forgotten, it was only a few months back that someone blasted this very palace." He looked up at each in turn then extricated his compact form from between the two men and strode to the door. "You leave in the morning. Be ready!" As he turned the knob, he glanced back and hissed, "Not to worry about sleeping arrangements. We have assigned you two *aunties* to the same quarters," and he slipped out.

"I do not like that man," Vladimir grumbled. Boris nodded in complete agreement.

позже

Following a traditional Sunday military review, the Tsar's party returned to the Palace and each of the participants went their separate ways. Vladimir attended to the office of the guard to report to the Lieutenant. After completing his formal duty (and personal care), he walked to the Imperial private rooms, where he anticipated spending the early afternoon with his charge before trekking over to the Conservatory of Music with Boris.

Upon entering the chamber, Vladimir did not see Alexander. This differed from the usual post-review procedure. The Tsar always went directly from the livery stable to his private rooms, performed his personal care, and sat waiting for Vladimir to arrive.

This particular day, His Imperial Majesty was not to be found. Vladimir looked in every dark-paneled alcove and cranny without success. The Tsar's military uniform lay on the floor, as if he had merely stepped out and left it. He approached the metal face of the tiled fireplace and found it cool to the touch.

With a growing sense of dread, Vladimir scrambled out to the hallway in an attempt to ask anyone if they had seen the Tsar. No one appeared directly, but a cadence of tapping footsteps crescendoed, announcing the approach of someone. The Chief-of-Staff rounded the corner.

"Dmitri Konstantinovich!" Vladimir blurted out, "I must report that I cannot find His Imperial Majesty in his chamber!" the guard's usual calm demeanor stripped away by fear.

One corner of the little bald man's mouth rose a tiny bit. "Calm yourself, Sergeant. His Imperial Majesty is visiting with the Princess. I just left them in her chambers," and he offered a hand in the direction from which he had just arrived.

"Thank you, Chief-of-Staff! Thank you very much!" The guard rushed off, creating a cacophonous clattering on the marble tiling.

"The pleasure is all mine," Dmitri said to himself with a smirky smile, "*Sergeant!*" and he hurried off.

When Vladimir reached the sitting room of the Princess, he stopped and took a few calming breaths to compose himself. Then he knocked at the door frame, "Your Highness?"

"Come in," came the muffled response, and Vladimir opened the door and entered as Catherine invited again,

"Come in, Sashka." The Princess lay naked on an over-stuffed red velour chaise lounge holding a square, hand-sized piece of pasteboard, her attention focused upon an array of other decorative cards on a table beside her. Even in her early 30s, Catherine had a slender and curvilinear body, with persimmon-sized breasts that had not yet given in to gravity.

She placed the fancy square on the table and then looked up. "Oh, my!" Catherine reached behind the chaise to retrieve a gauzy pink dressing gown that she used to cover herself.

"Your Highness!" Vladimir balked and averted his gaze. "My sincerest apologies. I had been instructed that His Imperial Majesty would be found here in your chambers."

While the guard covered his eyes with a gloved hand, the Princess stood and donned the gown unhurriedly, as if she actually wanted the young soldier to peer at her bare form. Once she had wrapped the nearly-sheer fabric around her body, Catherine announced, "All clear, Sergeant," with a change in tone that could have indicated a modicum of remorse.

Vladimir removed his hand from his eyes, and even though the frilly lace went all the way up to the chin of the Princess, he could still see the outline of her body through the insubstantial gown. He turned his head away.

"Sergeant," she admonished, "I'm surprised at you. Are you not married?"

"No, Your Highness," Vladimir dropped his gaze to the floor. "I serve His Imperial Majesty alone."

"Surely a handsome, young man such as you has seen women in a state of undress before," Catherine taunted. When he did not respond, she added, "Or perhaps not…" with a drop in pitch.

"Your Highness, gazing upon your unclothed body is not permitted. It is against protocol."

"Protocol!" she blasted. "How I hate hearing about protocol! You have rules for this, rules for that. Crawfish shall whistle on the mountain before it all makes sense to me. I am surprised you have not yet developed protocols for wiping one's *popka*!"

"Princess, where is His Imperial Majesty, if you please?" Vladimir inquired hastily.

Catherine's head pivoted about. "He was just here. Look at that uncompleted sketch." She pointed to a pad of paper on a table near the chaise.

The guard walked across the room and looked down at a blurry depiction of a naked woman. He quickly turned away and his gaze stopped at the array of cards next to the chaise.

"My Sashka likes to draw me in the nude," her intonation suggested flirtation. She followed the guard's focus. "Ah, I see you have an interest in the cards." Catherine sat on the lounge and sprawled. "An old gypsy woman named Minditsi gave me this set years ago, and I have always played at it for fun. Do you see any familiar images?"

The colorful squares had crossing diagonal lines diving each card into four triangles. Each triangle contained one half of an image. Some of the images lined up in the display on the table. Most obvious to Vladimir were a fox and a snake, which suggested a wily opponent and undetected deception.

Other familiar designs, such as the moon, a heart, a tree, a dagger, or fire, were divided from their matches. The Princess looked down at the arrangement, picked up one card and rotated it before placing it down again. This new positioning revealed a castle, but upside-down.

"Fascinating, yes?" she asked. "I just wish I could remember what these items portend. Minditsi instructed me in the ways of the cards, but I can no longer recall any of the meanings. How sad…" Catherine's eyes drifted up to those of the Sergeant gazing down. A distinct knock and click caused both of them to turn toward the door as 62-year-old Tsar Alexander entered in a silk housecoat and light cloth cap. "Sashka, my love," the Princess purred, "your handsome, young guard has done an excellent job of keeping me quite safe until you have finally returned to my side." She smiled up at Vladimir and winked with the eye Tsar Alexander could not see.

позже

Once he finished his morning responsibilities in the kitchen, Boris sought the services of the Royal tailor, whom Vladimir had mentioned he knew from the academy. The sight of a slender, somewhat effeminate, fellow with protuberant eyes, meandering hands, and a sweaty forehead that extended all the way back to the crown defied his expectations of someone who had graduated from the Page Corps. The new *chef de cuisine* explained that he had been requested by the Chief-of-Staff to obtain an appropriate set of clothes, and the tailor's wrinkle of a smile indicated his delight for sizing the kitchen chief up with a cloth measuring tape.

Boris had not experienced such intimate contact with someone before unless he had intended to continue on to more erotic activity. However, the touch of the long-fingered clothier on his torso and legs had unintended consequences, and the chef's member began to swell involuntarily. It took but a few seconds for the other fellow to discover this consequence, and he peered up with one hopeful eyebrow raised.

Without thinking about it, or realizing what signal it might send, Boris covered his crotch with both hands. The tailor exhaled heavily and continued his measuring duties.

When the kitchen chief returned to his suite, Vladimir stood looking back. Boris opened his mouth as if to relate his episode with the royal tailor, but he thought better of it and pursed his lips instead.

"Borushka? What is it?" Vladimir inquired.

Boris merely shook his head. "Nothing, Vovka."

The two men prepared for the evening ahead without any further conversation. Boris wore his *poddyovka*, and Vladimir chose a black *kosovorotka*[11] with a chain of red, embroidered flowers ringing the neck and sleeves. Because of the warmer summertime weather, neither brought a coat.

A slight salty breeze brushed their faces as they walked along the embankment of the Neva River. When they reached the meat pie vendor, Boris looked at Vladimir with a question on his face.

"No, thank you." Vladimir offered. "I made sure to grab something to eat at the Palace this time."

After they turned away from the river, Boris began the discussion he had eluded earlier. "You say you attended the academy with the Royal tailor?"

Vladimir nodded, "Yes."

Boris hesitated so that he could phrase his question without sounding too prying. "Were the two of you friends? Friendly, I mean." He looked at Vladimir for an answer.

"Friends? Of a sort, I suppose." The Sergeant walked facing forward. "We did not socialize at school events, only had a few classes with him." He turned to Boris. "Is there something you are attempting to ask me, Borushka?"

"Well… I didn't want to… It's just that —"

"Spit it out, please!" Vladimir commanded. "Just say it."

Boris stopped walking. "Did you… Were you two ever… intimate?"

Vladimir paused long enough to digest the question, then he broke forth in booming laughter.

"It's not funny, Vovka. That man has sticky fingers, and I don't know how I would feel if I knew he had them all over you." Boris had not intended to look pouty, but he achieved that goal without trying.

"Yes, I know Ilya Ivanovich has the eye for men, and his eyes do make the circuit, but—be assured—his 'sticky fingers,' as you put it, have only touched me in a professional manner in the due course of his Palace duties." He glanced at his downwardly-focused friend. "I did not realize you might be given to such jealousies, Borushka."

"I am glad to hear that, Vladimir Yuryevich." Boris faced forward and resumed walking. Once again they had reached the Potseluev Bridge. "I am not jealous. No, indeed. I merely wanted to… I mean… that man… it's just —"

"Not to worry, Borushka," Vladimir grasped Boris's hand and held it as they walked the rest of the way to the Conservatory.

As they approached the bland, brown building, the crowd of men who had huddled in the vestibule wearing overcoats and hats in the frigid February were now standing outside with summer suits and smiles. This time the circle of cultural friends welcomed Boris and Vladimir with hugs and *bisou* kisses.

"My darlings," Apukhtin gushed as he wrapped his bear-like arms around Vladmir. "How good to see you Palace boys again." Boris only received a lukewarm handshake. "We were just discussing that performance by Dostoyevsky at the Pushkin Memorial dedication. Were you there? Did you see it?"

Boris and Vladimir glanced at each other and then shook their heads in unison.

The oversized poet put his hands up to either side of his plump mouth. "Oh, my! What a diatribe!"

Some of the other men began to file into the building as Apukhtin continued his assessment of earlier events. "This Dostoyevsky—someone whom we have held in such high regard—so outspoken, so forceful!" He looked at Boris and Vladimir for a response, but the two of them just looked at each other, seemingly not knowing what to say. "As if he stood clutching the very dais at Church of the Vladimir Icon of the Mother of God delivering a Sunday homily. He declared the Roman Catholics have abandoned Christ, Protestants nothing but a hotbed of inbred snakes, and the poor, dogmatic fellow proclaimed our mother church the only true faith, the only one still loyal to our lord Jesus." Again, he paused for a response, but when none came forth, he continued on, "And he virtually committed high treason by espousing the socialistic society now popular in France!"

The impresario Stasov appeared at the door. "Aleksey Nikolayevich, please stop pestering our friends and come inside. The boy is about to start playing."

"Yes, Volodya, at once." He turned to Boris and Vladimir and spoke in a more hushed fashion, "Mark my words, that rabble-rousing Dostoyevsky will come to a bad end. He hardly even mentioned our beloved Pushkin for whom we had gathered to honor!" Apukhtin turned and waddled into the Conservatory.

Boris and Vladimir looked at each other, smiled in amusement, and followed the large fellow inside. In the performance hall, very few people other than the ones they knew occupied the chairs. The poet made his way toward the front to sit close to the piano. They sat toward the middle of the chamber.

A few moments later, three people stepped out from the hallway near the front of the room. The first, Madame Nadezhda von Meck, who wore a tight-fitting, dark-grey, high-collared, knee-length, dress with a few ruffles and many small buttons. Quite a handsome woman in her early 50s, her short, curly, still-dark hair framed a long, oval face. Following her, Pyotr Tchaikovsky, in a beige summer suit, and behind him a sullen-looking young fellow with chestnut hair in a crude bowl cut, a mangy van Dyke, and pale skin, wearing an ill-fitting, dark wool jacket. Tchaikovsky took an uncomfortable-looking seat next to Apukhtin.

Madame von Meck clasped her hands in front of her waist and began, "Thank you all for coming to our recital this afternoon. I want to introduce to you a young man we met in Paris who now gives piano lessons to my daughters and will soon be a musical force to reckon with in his own right." The surly young man bowed slightly and smiled tightly at his patron. "He shall begin with a few solo pieces by other composers, and then I will join him for a four-hand piece. Following that, our young protégé will demonstrate one of his own compositions, and I think you will all find his *nouveau* style most fascinating!" She smiled at the young man, and his eyes shifted away. "Patrons of the Conservatory, I now present to you, Achille-Claude Debussy of Paris!" Madame von Meck took a seat next to Tchaikovsky as the boy sat down at the keyboard to a light smatter of applause.

He began with a few movements of a Beethoven sonata, then a romance by Schumann, and a Chopin Ballade. The stylings leaned more toward light and airy, as opposed to the traditional heavy-handed Russian methods. During the performance, Tchaikovsky shifted in his seat frequently. It could have been the youngster's performance, it could have been the proximity of the poet seated next to him.

Madame von Meck joined Debussy on the bench and together they tackled the four-hand *Capriccio on Russian Themes* by Glinka. At the end of the piece, the patron stood and announced, "And now Monsieur Debussy will grace us with his own work, *Danse Bohémienne.*

Even before the woman had returned to her seat, the young man began pressing the keys again. The piece did not last very long, sounded vaguely Slavonic, hardly repeated itself, and had dissonant harmonies not common in Russian music.

Boris turned to his friend, "Well, what did you think of today's program?"

Vladimir turned his head one way and the other, "Again, I am probably not the best person to ask regarding music, but I did enjoy his… fresh approach to the classical pieces, and—of course—I adored the Glinka. However…" the guard's eyes darted about.

"I did not care much for his own composition either, Vovka. Do not trouble yourself trying to deliver kinder words." His head swiveled about. "I do not see the Grand Duke today. I wonder if he even received an invitation."

As they stood, Apukhtin and Tchaikovsky walked past, the poet in full critical mode, "… yes, but at least he made an attempt to sound somewhat Bohemian–in a French, Impressionistic kind of manner."

Tchaikovsky shook his head, "I am sorry, Aleksey Nikolayevich, but I must disagree. It may have been pretty, but it was much too short. Not a single idea was expressed fully, as would be expected in the style he attempted to reproduce. Its form was terribly shriveled, and it lacked any kind of unity."

"But it follows the current Impressionism movement in France. I adore their panache and audacity."

Tchaikovsky shook his head. "I, however, do not."

Apukhtin held up a flabby hand. "Then I guess we will have to disagree on this, Pyotr Ilyich. Oh, Stasov," who just happened by, "what did you think of young Debussy's composition?"

The impresario stopped, stared at Apukhtin and then turned to Tchaikovsky. "Did you enjoy it, Pyotr Ilyich?"

The composer fidgeted and glanced down. "No, Volodya, I must say I did not."

Stasov pointed at Tchaikovsky, "I agree with him," and he whisked away.

Before Boris and Vladimir could return to the entrance, Madame von Meck intercepted them with a sweeping sidelong movement. "Gentlemen. I had hoped to make your acquaintance before you returned to your little Palace." Her petite smile seemed to suggest an ulterior motive.

The two men paused, looked at each other, and then Vladimir turned to the lady, taking her hand. "Madame von

Meck," he kissed the back of her wrist, "a pleasure in meeting you, I'm sure." He let the hand drop, but instead of giving in to gravity, it drew up to her neck and then over to Boris, who stood frozen.

Vladimir elbowed him, and the chef duplicated his friend's hand-kissing gesture. "A pleasure, madam." He smiled at her and then at Vladimir.

"Please. We are all friends here. Just call me Nadya. You must come to my home for dinner this week," she purred as she retrieved her hand once again. "I shall be hosting an evening of culture and music. Tolstoy is going to read from Pushkin, Tchaikovsky and my young piano instructor will play."

"I'm sorry, madam," Vladimir spoke, and Madame von Meck prickled at the word. "Nadya. While it sounds thoroughly enjoyable, we have just been informed that His Imperial Majesty shall be traveling in the morning and we are both required to accompany him."

The lady bristled with eagerness. "How exciting! The two of you get to provide personal attention to His Imperial Majesty." Her voice wafted as if she were fantasizing about wayfaring with the Tsar herself.

"Perhaps when we return," Boris suggested, "if that meets with your ladyship's approval." Vladimir nodded.

Madame von Meck glanced at the chef with wide eyes. "Yes! That would be marvelous. I hope this shall occur before the season has ended. Any friends of Volodya are certainly friends of mine." She glanced and pointed at Stasov, who stood across the room speaking with Debussy. "Well, gentlemen, I bid you a fair journey." She curtseyed, the two men bowed slightly, and the lady waltzed over to where Stasov and Debussy stood.

"Well, Borushka," Vladimir turned to Boris, "we are making new friends, even if solely due to our association with His Imperial Majesty. I get the disquieting feeling Madame von Meck carries fire in one hand and water in the other."

They nodded in agreement as the two walked out of the chamber. As they exited, they noticed the crumpled form of Mussorgsky sitting in the back row, his eyes rheumy and glassy. A rosy, bulbous nose pointed up toward a corner of the ceiling, and his fingers waggled in rhythm, apparently enjoying music that no one else could hear.

Boris looked upon his old friend, the greatest Russian composer to that point, and sensed it might be the last time. He had to avert his gaze to avoid intensifying the grip of pain on his heart.

The following day, the Royal household prepared to take some time at Tsarskoe Selo. Peter the Great had given the property to his future wife Catherine, and when she became Empress, she developed the site into a country residence for the House of Romanov. The nation's first railway connected Tsarskoe Selo with St. Petersburg in 1837.

Two Imperial residences dominate the village: Catherine Palace and Alexander Palace. Each sat amidst a garden park and each had its own style. Catherine Palace appeared more Baroque and antique, while Alexander Palace had more modern, but Neoclassical, appointments.

Alexander Palace, Tsarskoe Selo

"This room is so small compared to ours back in St. Petersburg," Boris remarked upon entering their temporary quarters.

"Alexander Palace is much older. They made due with smaller chambers. Perhaps the kitchen will be more to your liking, Borushka."

"I certainly hope so." Boris looked across the room at the dashing young guard. He sighed audibly.

"Yes?" Vladimir responded.

"Oh, nothing, my friend. Sometimes I have to keep reminding myself that Moscow wasn't built all in one day."

Vladimir smiled. "No, that it was not. What is taking too much time for your penchant, Borushka? Is it something I can assist with?"

Boris clenched his fists and then relaxed. "No, Vovka. It is something I must deal with on my own, but I appreciate your offer."

The guard bowed in an official manner. The chef laughed.

"Thank you for amusing me, Vovka," and the guard bent at the waist again, drawing another chuckle. "Tell me," Boris went on, "do you understand the reason we have conveyed ourselves all the way out here?"

Vladimir began removing personal articles and clothing from his travel bag. "From what I have been told, His

Imperial Majesty is working with Count Loris-Melikof to draw up some kind of plan to restructure the government."

"I hope that does not include removing us from our posts." Boris began unpacking as well.

"While I do not know any details, I have heard the two discussing a few ideas as they have walked together."

"Our glorious Tsar has released the serfs from slavery. What else could his subjects want?"

"The Count has expressed concern that the recent attempt to take the life of His Imperial Majesty demonstrates the people's uneasiness."

"I suppose they don't hit you in the nose for asking."

"From what I've heard, some are in a rush to have Russia be more like a Greek democracy, and they're willing to risk being hit in the nose, as you say. I hope they can learn to temper their aggravation because, as you know, Moscow was not built all in one day."

"Yes, so I have heard, Vovka." Boris had finished emptying his bag. "I believe I would like to inspect the kitchen facilities. Would you like to join me?"

"No, I think I will take the time to familiarize myself with the rest of the building and check in with my Lieutenant. I shall look forward to seeing you later. Let us hope that the cooking facilities here are up to your strict Parisian standards." He smiled.

"Yes, let us hope."

They walked toward the door, but Boris stopped and turned abruptly, "Vovka, do you have an idea as to why Dmitri Konstantinovich did not accompany the rest of us on this journey?"

Vladimir reached for the handle, pulling the door open, "I suppose he needed to stay in St. Petersburg to oversee the household there. Why do you ask?"

"It just seems to me that he manages to turn up, wherever we happen to be, for better or for worse. I feel between the hammer and anvil most of the time with him, as if every-thing I say is wrong. I manage to anger him–unintentionally, of course–at every turn."

"Perhaps he is envious of your good looks," Vladimir smiled, Boris frowned. "Honestly, I can't think of a good rea-son for him to treat you so. You carry out your position most admirably."

"But he–oh, thank you for saying that–the man tends to find harm and insult with just about every action and word."

"Then let me suggest he might be upset with you for some-thing you did, and it might be something you are not aware of, and he takes every opportunity to extract his petty venge-ance, even though that little toad is quite distant from the ideals of perfection himself."

"It is easier to see the tiny mote in the eye of another than the large log in your own."

"Yes, I have heard that." Vladimir held the door open and indicated with his hand, "Shall we?"

Boris clasped the muscular arm of the guard and nodded slowly. "Thank you, Vovka," and they walked out into the narrow hallway.

While at Alexander Palace, the Tsar and Count Loris-Melikof continued to draft their plans to further modernize their country in hopes of keeping up with the developing Western European powers. Russia had already found itself behind the times with its outmoded military during the Crimean War, and Alexander II had no intentions of standing still while the rest of the world progressed around him.

---

[5] 1 Versta = 1 Km or 3500 ft.

[6] 1 Dyuim = 2.5 cm or 1 in.

[7] Due to its proximity to the North Pole, St. Petersburg experiences long hours of daylight around the Summer Solstice, with sunset not occurring until as late as 22:00. The festivities include fireworks and much comradery.

[8] Tsesarevich specifically refers to the heir apparent. Any son of a Tsar is called Tsarovich.

[9] Originally constructed as a barracks for the Lithuanian Regiment, the building became a prison in the 1820s.

[10] Originally governor-general of Lower Volga, Tsar Alexander appointed him Chief of the Supreme Administrative Commission to deal with the escalation in terrorism following the assassination attempt that February.

[11] A typical "peasant shirt" with a high, tabless collar, offset neck opening and long sleeves.

A STORYBOOK ROMANCE *hinges upon an event that propels two people together into intimacy. They may have been heading gradually toward each other already, but some pivotal moment in time accelerates their growing closer. Sometimes it is a random meeting, an unexpected tender encounter, or even Mother Nature herself. Every so often, it is a critical historic event.*

Tsar Alexander II continued to meet with Count Loris-Melikof, and the two great men worked on a ground-breaking document that would improve the relationship between the Russian rulers and the people they governed. Their proposed edict would further reform the bureaucracy by creating commissions composed of both government officials and private citizens, opening the tightly-closed doors of the regime to the public. This proclamation would usher in a new Russia, one poised to be on par with the increasingly modern democratic nation states of Europe.

But History had a different course in mind for the peoples of Russia…

Section Three:
Wonderful Things

March 1881
Alexander Palace, St. Petersburg

"Oh, finally! There you are!" Vladimir exclaimed as he opened the door to the shared suite. A head of blond curls hovered over the writing desk at the far end, under the window. Boris sat going through various piles of correspondence. "I first went to the kitchen, but they told me you had returned to our room."

"Yes, I needed some time to catch up on my letters." He turned around, briefly smiled, and then went back to the mound of papers. "This position has overwhelmed my daily routine, and I wanted to return a few of these before I have to go back to work." The promotion to Kitchen Chief had kept Boris very busy, and he hardly saw Vladimir for days at a time.

The guard, in his formal outfit, shiny and glistening, stepped in further. "I am glad to have found you. There is an official duty I must perform later today, and I wanted to know if you wished to accompany me."

Boris swiveled to catch the gaze of his friend. "Me? With *you* on official business?" one hand rested daintily on his breastbone.

"Yes, you," Vladimir chuckled at the mock outrage. "As it turns out, our dearest… dearest society friend," he rolled his eyes, "Madame Nadya von Meck," and he raised his nose, which made his plumed hat start to fall. He had to reach up and steady it. "She has invited Her Majesty, Princess Catherine, to an art showing this afternoon at her home, and the Princess has requested my services as her personal attendant."

The chef swiveled back to the desk, grasped a letter from the top of a stack, turned back round and held the paper up.

"What is that?" questioned Vladimir.

"An invitation from Madame von Meck herself for the two of us to attend the showing this afternoon."

"Oh."

Boris pouted. "Vovka, you and I so rarely see each other lately, we have gotten far behind in our getting on."

"Yes, I agree. Are you free to attend with me?"

"Quite." He nodded. "I did not have a chance to ask if *you* would be interested."

Vladimir looked away. "While I would always welcome the chance to spend more time with you," he returned his gaze to Boris, "I am not sure I would want that time to be spent in the presence of Madame von Meck. That woman annoys me."

"Really? How so?"

"First off, she twirls her tongue more than a cow swirls its tail." The guard shrugged his shoulders and shuffled from foot to foot. "I am not sure how to explain this fully, but I always feel like she wants to get into bed with the Tsar and the Princess. You and I are but the chambermaids she needs to appease in order to obtain her majestic wishes."

"Oh, my! You really believe she wants to sleep with the Royal couple?"

"Ha, ha!" the Guard laughed. "Goodness, no! Just an expression. I believe that Nadya has aspirations to associate more personally with His Imperial Majesty and the Princess."

"Ah, I see now." He returned the letter to the desk. "Yes, she does seem a bit *too* familiar with us when we are in her presence."

"Exactly! But now I am ordered to accompany Her Highness into Nadya's lair, and I am happy to hear that you have been invited as well. What is the occasion? Does the invitation specify?"

Boris placed his hand on his breast again. "The artist Repin has completed a portrait of our dearly departed friend Mussorgsky, and the reception is for the unveiling."

"I am not familiar with this Repin or his works, Borushka. Is he well-known?"

"As known as unknown, I surmise." He pushed his lower lip forward and tipped his head from side to side. "All I can tell you is that he spent the last year in Zaporozhia[12] making studies for some new piece." Then he raised his upturned palms. "Oh, I will need some time to meet with Dmitri Konstantinovich. He wants to hear news of Little Mishka."[13]

"Little Mishka," Vladimir mocked. "Hmmmmmm."

Boris rolled his eyes. "Well, that's what the Chief-of-Staff calls him. It's difficult to believe the baby is almost a year old already. As they say, time flies."

"And speaking of time, I shall return in two hours. Please prepare yourself to ride in the open carriage."

Boris stood. "The open carriage? What an honor. What a privilege!"

"Yes," the guard smirked slightly, "you should be honored."

An envelope flew across the room missing the guard by an arm's-length.

"And perhaps we can get you some target practice as well." Vladimir slipped out the door quickly.

Before he had taken two steps, a curly-topped young man in a miniature sailor's costume bumped into him. It was Nicholas, the 12-year-old son of the Tsesarevich. A gilt-edged book within an inlaid wood cover fell to the tiled floor with a clatter, and the boy tumbled down. Vladimir reached for the book and found it had nothing but blank pages.

"Hey, aren't you my grandfather's guard?" Nicholas accused. "Give me back my book!" He raised himself off the floor in a spidery manner.

"What is this, Nicholas Alexandrovich? It has no story, no pictures."

"*That,*" the young man said as he snatched it from the guard's hands, "is my souvenir book! Mama just gave it to me and told me to fill it with wonderful things." His satiny, smug smile could easily annoy others. He ran off hugging the new treasure to his chest.

позже

When Boris arrived at the Chief-of-Staff's office, the door stood ajar, but he knocked on the doorframe just in case.

Dmitri Konstantinovich looked up from his desk, "Ah, Boris Mikhailovich, please come in."

As a fly braving a spider's web, the kitchen chief entered the room with extreme caution.

"Sit. Tell me all about little Mishka."

Boris sat in the chair near the desk. "There isn't anything new to tell you since my mother's last letter. She and Auntie Oksana seem to enjoy having a little one to take care of, and, as they are sharing the burden, it has proved less difficult than expected."

"That is good! Excellent news."

"Is that all, sir?"

"No." He picked up a pen but put it down again. "Boris Mikhailovich, Mishka is of great significance to me. You may not have realized this, but he is my only living relative. That is why any news of him is of major importance to me."

"Yes, I see now. I had not grasped the situation entirely." Boris shifted in the chair. The atmosphere of unresolved tension hung thickly in the office.

"When my sister died, I lost half my family. I feel rather alone now." He spread his hands apart over the desk. "On another matter," Dmitri Konstantinovich turned and stared directly at the Kitchen Chief, "news has reached my ear that you frequent a certain Turkish bath at Znamensky. Is this not true?"

Boris flinched upon hearing the words. "Sir, I believe what I do during my time off is my business, not –"

"As a Rank member of the Tsar's household, your behavior is my business at all hours, Kitchen Chief, including those you spend with a certain young fellow who goes by the name of 'Igor.'"

Again, Boris flinched, hearing the boy's name. "Sir, is there a problem with my leisure activities?"

"Problem? Not for me. I do wish to maintain a certain level of decorum among my staff, but–as you say–these things occur during your own personal time." One of his eyebrows arched to its limit. "My only concern is what should happen if your Sergeant heard of your nighttime dalliances. How would Vladimir Yuryevich react to this information?" His face displayed pouting lips, upturned nose and half-lidded eyes.

Another flinch at yet another name. "If I may, how do you even know my whereabouts during my private time? Are you having me followed?"

The Chief-of-Staff smiled with a greasy, flattened grin. "It appears you are not the only person in this household who knows 'Igor,' an enterprising fellow who gives a certain satisfaction for only a few rubles."

"And are you holding this information against me for some reason? For what purpose do you tell me this?"

"Ah, the reason–you ask. Well, Boris Mikhailovich, you arrived out of nowhere, placed by our superiors in my employ without first giving me any say in the matter. Since that time you have ingratiated yourself with the Royal family, and, at times, used that favor to coerce my decision-making to your own desires." His face reddened to the point of glowing. "Through circumstances beyond my control, you are now the Kitchen Chief and your mother is raising my nephew. Young man, it seems you are attempting to jump above your head, and that is simply not tolerable." Dmitri paused for a deep breath. "Suffice it to say there may be times in the future when I might need a favor or two from you. I am hoping that my keeping your private matters private will help… motivate you to accede to my requests. Does that make things clearer, Kitchen Chief?"

"Very! You are threatening to tell Vladimir Yuryevich about my personal activities unless I agree to submit to your personal whims." He stood up briskly.

"Yes, I guess that is one way of looking at it. You see, Boris Mikhailovich, you have been in the kitchen for quite a while, and now you must eat what you have cooked, as the saying goes." A self-righteous smile spread all the way across his weasel-like face. "Do we have an understanding?"

Boris glared at the smug little man. "Is that all, sir?"

"Yes, I believe so for now," Dmitri Konstantinovich beamed. "Do shut the door on your way out."

позже

"Sergeant, please explain to me why this man is sitting in the carriage with us instead of up front next to the driver," Princess Catherine commanded as the royal sleigh pulled out of the Palace courtyard.

"He is Boris Mikhailovich, Princess, the Kitchen Chief."

"You are the Kitchen Chief?" She studied his pink face and green eyes.

"Yes, Your Highness." Boris felt a bit uncomfortable with both having to speak directly to Princess Catherine and the texture of his new gabardine suit. "I oversee the preparation of all the meals for you and His Imperial Majesty."

"I apologize for my patronizing inquiry, but it seemed out of the ordinary to have someone I had not met before riding in the passenger compartment with me. Please allow me to say that I have truly enjoyed the cuisine at the Palace. And your name again?"

"Boris Mikhailovich, Your Highness."

"And your family name, if you please?"

"Zelany." He bundled his coat a bit tighter as a breeze along the Embankment chilled the air.

Catherine looked up into the clear, azure sky and then back at Boris. "I am not familiar with that name. Where are your people from, Boris Mikhailovich?"

"Tula, Your Highness."

"Ah, but your culinary skills do not come from Tula, a region more associated with samovars than fine dining."[14]

"No, Your Highness. I trained in Paris."

"Marvelous. I just adore French cooking. *Ah, la belle cuisine de la belle France.* No wonder I have enjoyed your food so." The Princess turned her attention to Vladimir. "And how do the two of you know each other?"

It took a moment to respond as Vladimir had been observing the other carriages along the riverfront roadway. "Your Highness, I share a room with the Kitchen Chief at the Palace."

"And yet he is riding in our coach to the home of Madame von Meck with us?"

"Boris Mikhailovich and I are social acquaintances of our hostess. He was also a friend of the composer Mussorgsky. She has invited us both to attend."

The Princess turned to look at the Summer Garden as they passed. Small buds on the trees had begun to form. She then spoke to Boris. "Have you been to the home of Madame von Meck before?"

"Yes, Your Highness. We met last year at the Conservatory of Music and she has occasionally requested our attendance." He smiled at Vladimir.

Catherine studied the silent interaction between the two men. "I see. Well, then." Her eyes shifted first to the guard, then down at her lap and then to Boris. "You are no ordinary Kitchen Chief, Boris Mikhailovich from Tula, given that you have made the acquaintance of both the departed and our hostess."

"As a matter of fact, Your Highness, it was in Paris that I first made the acquaintance of Modeste Petrovich as well as the Grand Duke, your stepson. It was Sergei Alexandrovich who invited me to work in the Palace kitchen because of a dessert I had prepared in his honor while I worked at *Café Anglais*."

"Oh, which dessert was that?"

"*Soufflé à la Russe*, Your Highness."

"Is that the one with the rich gingery taste?" Boris nodded. "I so enjoy that. Your people in Tula do like their ginger root, don't they?" Boris nodded again. Catherine's eyes narrowed as she turned her head away and she peered sidelong at the chef. "Do you ever prepare food for Madame von Meck's affairs?"

"No, Your Highness. I only serve the House of Romanov and no others."

"Please let us keep it that way. I want your gastronomic delights to be ours, and ours alone!" She turned back, reached across and placed a fur-trim-gloved hand on Boris's knee.

Boris turned to Vladimir, who looked directly forward. The Princess smiled and slowly pulled her hand back. The three rode on with only the sound of clopping horse hooves on the cobblestones.

A few minutes later, the royal coach stopped in front of a brownstone mansion along Zakharevskaya Street, a three-story home with a plain façade. Vladimir hopped down and gave a visual scan of the area. When his sense of security had been satisfied, he reached up for the Princess. She took the guard's hand with one of hers and scooped up the layers of fabric in her skirt with the other. Boris followed behind.

As they reached the front door, the impresario Vladimir Stasov walked up. "Your Highness," he bowed, took her hand and gently kissed it. "Boris Mikhailovich, Vladimir Yuryevich, how nice to see you both again." His eyes paused on the guard as he had never seen him in his military outfit previously. With a smile, he held the door for the Princess and her two men.

Inside, servants took their overcoats, and the entryway opened into a large sitting room with a high, arched, carved-wood ceiling. From the center hung a sparkling chandelier as large as a grand piano. The parqueted floor revealed an intricate, maze-like pattern, and large tapestries hung between the double doors along the side walls. At the far end of the room, the young Debussy sat playing parlor music quietly. His blank expression and pursed lips suggested a desire to be elsewhere.

Tables had been moved to the walls, and heavy, wooden chairs set in rows for the guests. Atop the tables sat small easels with canvases, but one great easel at the end of the room held a cloth-covered piece.

Members of the Peredvizhniki (a group referred to as the 'Itinerants' because they took their works on tours about the country), presented their latest pieces. Each artist stood by his painting. The crowd circulated throughout the room, observing, pointing, discussing. Boris and Vladimir flanked the Princess as she walked about, peering at the works and nodding to other guests. Even though she had been married to their Tsar for almost a year, not everyone had yet accepted her as a replacement for their Tsaritsa.

Madame von Meck, in a garish and sprawling frilly frock, breezed into the room and directly up to Catherine. "Your Highness," she bowed deeply, making the crinoline hoops clack against each other, "Welcome to my humble abode." She straightened up like a ballerina in third position, her sweeping arm presenting and displaying the room with a final flick of the wrist.

The Princess extended her hand to Nadya, who quickly grasped and kissed the glove. "Madame von Meck, we appreciate your invitation. The Tsar and I are particularly interested in the great artists of our nation. And, please, call me Catherine."

Madame von Meck's eyes bulged and her face lengthened in surprise. "Yes! By all means. And you must call me Nadya." She bowed again.

"Thank you, Nadya." The Princess smiled.

"Excuse me… Catherine," Nadya grinned like a girl with a secret, "I must go retrieve our guest of honor. I shall return momentarily."

The Princess nodded curtly, and Madame von Meck exited through one of the sets of double doors.

Vladimir turned to Boris, "I believe she got what she wanted." Boris nodded.

The three of them strolled the room and stopped at Shiskin's *Morning in a Pine Forest,* which displayed three bear cubs and their mother frolicking among storm-broken pine trees lit by crepuscular light. The artist did not approach them. When gazing upon Levitsky's *Portrait of a Village Girl*, the Princess shuddered at the image of a plain-clothed young woman standing in a storage room holding some sort of odd hook on a stick.

Before they were able to move on, Madame von Meck returned, holding Ilya Repin's hand. His green eyes darted beneath the dangling shocks of dark hair. A wispy mustache and detached goatee slightly covered his puckering lips.

"Bonjour," Nadya attempted to say, but her Russian pronunciation made it sound more like "bawn-zhur." She moved toward the covered painting on the easel. *"Mesdames, messieurs, s'il vous plaît."* Her arms indicated the chairs, and people began to sit. A house servant escorted the Princess, Boris and Vladimir to the front row, and a smiling hostess beamed at her prized guests.

"Achille-Claude, if you please," the hostess called across the hall, and the young man played a few more measures before ceasing the serenade. She then addressed the assembled guests, "I have invited you here today," her eyes traveled to a few of the people, ending with the Princess, and a grand smile, "to enjoy the works of our traveling artists, and—in particular—a new, and quite timely, portrait of our recently-departed national treasure, a musical genius for the ages, Modeste Petrovich Mussorgsky." A few people applauded politely. *"Monsieur* Repin began shortly before the composer's death and completed the work just last week." Nadya stepped to the concealed canvas. *"Mes amis, je vous présente..."* and she flicked her wrist, gently tugging at the muslin covering to reveal the portrait.

Silence.

Instead of an homage to one of the country's most beloved composers, perhaps a youthful, vibrant version of him seated at a piano furiously playing one of his many popular works, or even leading an orchestra with a baton, it appeared to be an ailing man merely sitting for a portrait. While an honest and true depiction, it could not be considered flattering. His auburn hair looked unkempt, flying off at strange angles, the nose depicted like a reddened potato. A rather plain, dark green housecoat with a wide, red lapel appeared unwashed and disheveled. Only the sidelong glance of bright, shiny grey-blue eyes gave life to the otherwise dreary work.

After a few seconds, someone coughed. Both Nadya and Repin craned their necks, gazing about the non-responsive crowd. Madame von Meck began clapping insistently and others eventually joined in, somewhat reluctantly. She turned to the painter. He snapped his chin upward and disappeared through the doors from which they had entered.

People began to stand and walk toward the refreshment tables. The young Debussy began playing a Bach Partita. Madame von Meck approached the Princess.

"Your Highness—Catherine—may I get you something to drink or eat?" Her pretentious smile crinkling the face powder.

"Thank you, but no," the Princess stood, assisted by Vladimir. "I only eat food prepared by my loyal chef," and she turned to Boris, who stood and bowed. "However, we can share a bottle of sweet sherry, but only if it has never been opened and you take the first drink." She returned the smile.

Nadya froze for a moment and then responded, "Of course, of course! This way, please," and she indicated one of the sets of double doors. Vladimir accompanied the ladies, but Stasov, who stood nearby observing the interaction, pulled Boris aside before he could follow the others.

"You were one of Modeste's favorites, and I just wanted you to know I was with him when he passed." The chef nodded somberly. "We had to place him in the military hospital following an 'attack'," he mimicked drinking, "and I brought him an apple for his health." Boris smiled. "When I arrived at his room, he sat clutching a small bottle of cognac, poised to drink the spirits, which had been strictly forbidden by his doctors."

"Forbidden because the alcohol could bring on another 'attack'?"

"Yes," Stasov nodded. "I asked how he obtained such a thing, and he told me he had to bribe a guard with 25 rubles–*25 rubles*! Where does he even get such money?" His head shook back and forth. "He took the apple and began chewing ravenously. When he offered me the bottle, I politely refused–of course–but before I could wrestle the darned thing away from him, he had swallowed it all in one gulp. Within seconds he began twitching and convulsing. I yelled for the doctors. 'Modeste!' I called, 'What have you done?' He began sobbing and cried, 'Ah, I am a wretch! It is all over.' By the time the doctors arrived, he lay silent and still. Rimsky-Korsakov is so upset. He kept asking Modeste to set his piano compositions on paper, and now he will have to reconstruct them from memory." A tear formed in the corner of the impresario's eye. "The first of my Mighty Five[15] to succumb."

Boris reached up and put a comforting hand on the tall man's shoulder.

"A great loss," Stasov declared, "a great loss to us all." He turned and walked to view the all-too-realistic portrait just as the portly poet Apukhtin stepped up. Boris followed.

"Such a tragedy, do you not think so, Volodya?" The big man pulled a large red silk handkerchief from a pocket and dabbed at his sorrowful eyes. "So soon after the loss of Dostoyevsky. How many other deaths must we suffer this season?"

Stasov stood focused on the two-dimensional depiction of his old friend. "It is incredible!" he muttered, "Simply incredible!"

позже

That night, when Vladimir returned to the suite following his Saturday evening duties, Boris sat writing, his back facing the door. The guard lifted a finger and opened his mouth slightly, as if to once again admonish his friend for maintaining that vulnerable position.

"Yes, I know you would prefer it if I did not arrange myself thusly, but I enjoy looking out the window while I go through my correspondence."

The finger lowered, "Even at night?" Vladimir began arranging blankets on the floor.

"Even at night." Boris turned around and watched the bed-making activity. "Vovka, you have slept on that floor for nearly a year now. Is it not getting uncomfortable?"

Vladimir dropped the pillows. "A good soldier can sleep anywhere. Floor, barracks, feather bed…," he pointed to the nook where Boris slept.

"Then if it's all the same," the chef stared at the guard, "why not sleep in the 'feather bed,' as you call it?" and he pointed to the nook as well.

"Borushka," Vladimir squatted upon his makeshift mattress, "my choice of sleeping arrangement has nothing to do with you," he looked up into the other's dewy eyes, "but rather with me." Boris raised an eyebrow. "I prefer to have my own bed, if it pleases you to know."

"It does not *please* me, Vovka," the words sounded harsher than necessary. "As we seem to be sharing the same room, the same air–and just about the same life," he flung his arms about to indicate the various things, "it would seem almost natural for us to share the same bed."

"So it would seem… to you." Vladimir sat down and began to cover himself with a blanket as Boris looked on with longing. "But I ask your further indulgence in allowing me the necessary time to arrive at your particular level of comfort. Having lived a life of military solitude, I find the intimacy you propose takes much longer for me to develop."

"Intimacy?" came the echo. "I have not proposed marriage to you. Only that we share a mattress large enough for two. That is all, Vovka."

Vladimir lay back and rolled away from the lamp on the writing desk. "If that is all, Borushka, then let me be the one to decide when the time is right to act upon that option. Please." He fluffed the pillow one more time before lying his head down. "And do extinguish the light when you are finished. Thank you."

позже

The next morning, Vladimir woke to find Boris still asleep. He quietly put his bedclothes away and snuck out of their room without disturbing the snoring chef.

Something on his mind had caused him to awaken early. The previous night he had most likely hurt Boris's feelings by not complying with his request to share the bed. However, he knew that he was not yet ready to become more involved, despite having shared these intimate quarters for many months now. It was the closest he had allowed himself to be with another person to whom he was not related. Yet he still had a halfhearted fear of becoming entangled emotionally.

Unaware of what held him back, and unwilling to consider his reasoning or his options in that moment, Vladimir decided to focus on the duties of the day at hand. As it was Sunday, the Tsar would be taking his weekly ride to Mikhailovsky Manège for the customary troop review. After the unfortunate defeat in the Crimea 25 years previously,

∗ 143 ∗

Russia had endeavored to modernize its army. Most recently, victory over the Ottomans demonstrated a superiority that His Imperial Majesty wished to maintain.

Following the day's briefing, Vladimir assisted the Tsar into the fortified coach with the customary pomp and fanfare. That day, the Lieutenant of the Royal Guard joined with Vladimir and one other guard.

For some reason, perhaps nostalgia, 63-year-old Alexander had chosen to wear the outfit of the Sapper Battalion, a dark blue tunic with two columns of silver buttons, silver epaulettes and cords, and a dark helmet with a metal spike on top. It had been the Sapper Battalion who had saved his father and the Palace during an uprising when the Tsar was only seven years old.

Upon the death of Tsar Alexander I in December 1825, it had been presumed that his brother, Konstantin, would have succeeded him. When Konstantin renounced his claim in order to remain Governor of Poland, Alexander's son Nicholas assumed the throne. Thousands of military men objected to this succession as they had already sworn their allegiance to Konstantin. Almost 3,000 troops stood at Peter's Square and protested, while at the same time a grenadier squad attempted to capture the Winter Palace, where Nicholas and his family resided. After a thwarted cavalry charge against the rebels failed due to icy cobblestones, the new Tsar ordered artillery bombardments, which devastated the attackers and eventually drove them away.

The parade of carriages and sleighs proceeded on its usual route. As they rode along the Embankment, an open sleigh carrying Tsesarevich Alexander Alexandrovich and his son, Nicholas, passed in the opposite direction, presumably headed to the Palace. Vladimir thought back to the encounter with the young man the previous day and his new prized possession, a blank book. The early-morning sunlight reflected off of the father's bald scalp, creating a small halo in the remnants of the fog.

After the minor spectacle of marching in formation and imitating gun noises in the old enclosure, the Tsar and his entourage got back into their vehicles to return to the Palace. A small crowd of people had assembled at the Pevchesky Bridge, which crosses the Catherine Canal just outside the Manège. Some of them began to wave to their monarch, and the stately Alexander returned the gesture from within the safety of the wheeled metal case.

On the approach of the bridge, a young blonde woman pulled a white lace handkerchief from her coat and waved it above her head vigorously. Suddenly, one of the men lobbed a cloth-wrapped object at the feet of the horses drawing the Royal carriage. As the metal box passed over it, the package exploded, knocking some of the onlookers down. The carriage shook forcefully, and the driver fell to the ground while the bomber ran away yelling, "There he goes! Get him!" The procession halted abruptly, and the crowd stared about with wide eyes, crossing themselves. A boy carrying a basket of meat lay groaning. Several people scurried off.

The Tsar rose from his seat and looked out the window. People scrambled to help the injured, and one of the Cossacks screamed in agony. As Alexander reached for the door handle, Vladimir urged, "Your Majesty, I suggest you stay inside where it is safe."

Ignoring the advice of his body guard, the Tsar stepped out and down to the ground, looking about at the damage caused by the small bomb. He crossed himself. The Lieutenant of the Guard, Alexei Andreyevich, rushed after him, Vladimir remained in the doorway at the top of the steps and admonished, "Your Majesty, please return to the carriage. It is not safe here. Let *us* look after the injured. Please." Once again, Alexander rejected the guard's appeal and walked around, surveying the casualties. As he walked toward the rear of the carriage, he slipped on one of the bloodied cobblestones, and the Lieutenant caught and steadied him. At the rear of the box, the two men examined the minor damage caused by the explosion.

From the sidelines, a woman in a heavy wool coat cried out, "The Tsar is unharmed! Thank God!" The Lieutenant then moved to stand between Alexander and the remaining crowd.

One man shouted back, "It is too early to thank God!" He held up what looked like a frosted Easter cake and flung it at the Tsar's feet and ran off. As the object hit the ground, it exploded, fragments spraying in every direction. When the smoke abated, Vladimir could see Alexander splayed out and attempting to prop himself up with his right arm, his shiny helmet nearby. The guard stepped down from the carriage, knelt over the Tsar and observed one of the eyes shut, the other staring blindly. He started to lift him, not realizing the extent of the trauma. As he raised Alexander's body, the lower parts of his legs remained on the ground, shattered hopelessly, drenched in the blood pouring out. Next to him lay the hopelessly immobile carcass of the Lieutenant, who apparently gave his life for the man he had served.

People screamed in fear and anger as they began crowding around the downed monarch. "The Tsar is dead!" "The Poles did it!" "Kill the Poles!" The remaining guards attempted to disperse the crowd, and the angry mob continued to chant as they scattered chaotically.

One of the accompanying sleigh drivers waved at Vladimir and caught his attention. The guard lifted and carried the broken torso as best he could, laid it on the floor of the sleigh and then climbed in. "Take him to the military hospital!"

Alexander looked up with the one eye and grasped Vladimir's arm. Once the guard looked directly at him, the Tsar shook his head.

"The palace?"

Alexander nodded and then lay back down.

"Hold on!" Vladimir cried to the driver. "His Imperial Majesty would prefer his own rooms."

The driver lashed the horses and they were on their way. Vladimir looked back and saw fragments of clothing, epaulets, sabers, and bloody chunks of human flesh on the bridge roadway. A nearby gas lamp pole had been bent by the blast, and it pointed like a ghostly finger toward the Palace.

The guard found a few blankets on one of the seats and wrapped what was left of the Tsar's legs. "Lie still, Your Majesty. We are taking you home." Alexander nodded and made a little smile. Vladimir held onto his fading master and prayed for the first time in many years.

As the speeding sleigh neared the entryway to the Palace, footmen approached. Their quizzical looks suggested that the news had not yet reached them. Dmitri Konstantinovich, in a woolen coat with brown fur collar and matching peaked fur cap, happened to be walking by and noticed the oddity. He ran up to the vehicle and asked Vladimir, "What has happened?" When the Chief-of-Staff first looked upon the pitiful condition of the Tsar, he turned his head and vomited uncontrollably on the cobblestones. "Get him to his rooms! I shall call for the doctor and a priest," and he ran off.

The footmen, driver, and Vladimir carried the mutilated body into Alexander's private rooms and placed him on the bed. Soon after, members of the family rushed in to see what had happened. Princess Catherine stood just outside the door, half-dressed, one hand on the wall, the other over her mouth. The Tsesarevich, tall and thickset, stood inside the room as far from Catherine as possible, staring at his dying father, arms folded across his ribcage, a stern expression on his face. His son Nicholas stood directly in front of him, clasping the wooden-bound book to his chest. A hubbub of mumbled prayers reverberated in the chamber.

Lying upon the Tsar's rattling chest was the Grand Cross medal awarded him by the King of Prussia in 1878. Only five such honors had been granted to those whose actions caused the retreat or defeat of an entire army. It was one of his favorite possessions, and he always wore it on troop review days.

The physician, Sergei Petrovich Botkin, arrived and began to attend the wounded Tsar. Alexander's left leg ended just above the knee, and the right just above the ankle. The doctor tested pulses at various points–neck, wrists, legs–and his head kept shaking back and forth. "Where is the priest?" he demanded "We have but maybe 15 minutes at the most."

Upon hearing the proposed death sentence, Catherine rushed in, fell onto her husband's chest and began wailing, "Sasha! Sasha!" The eldest son, Alexander, nodded to his youngest brother, Paul, who then escorted their disheveled step-mother back to her rooms.

People in the room wept and held onto each other. A tall, slender man in black woolen robes with shoulder-length greying hair and beard appeared at the door of the room. His steely eyes looked around until he caught sight of the Tsesarevich. He stepped in, clasping several sheets of official-looking papers.

A few minutes later Father Bazhenov arrived and shooed everyone from the chamber. As they exited, the lanky stranger handed the papers to the son Alexander, who glanced at the documents, tore them crosswise twice, scrunched up the pieces and quickly put them in his coat pocket as the two walked off together in silence along the darkened hallway. Nicholas followed them like a miniature shadow.

Vladimir watched as they disappeared around a turn, then he looked down at his bloodied uniform and wept. He prayed and cried some more for the man who had been his father figure, commander, sovereign, and friend. After a while, the sobbing subsided sufficiently and he slowly marched to the barracks to make his official report.

позже

When the door to the room opened, Boris startled awake and sat up in bed. "Who is there?" he called out.

As Vladimir stepped in, it seemed like a bad dream. His friend's uniform looked tattered and bloody. Just to make sure it was not as he saw, Boris rubbed his eyes while he heard the door shut. When he looked again, the scene had not changed. The guard's appearance suggested he had been in hand-to-hand battle. Boris leapt off the bed and hugged Vladimir tightly.

Once their bodies connected, Vladimir began sobbing and moaning.

"What is wrong, Vovka? What is it?"

The guard looked down into the other's green eyes, "Oh, Borushka, it is horrible!"

"What, Vovka? What is horrible?"

Instead of answering the question, Vladimir leaned in and began pressing his lips against Boris's mouth, hugging him even tighter.

"Vovka!" the chef exclaimed as he pulled his head back. "What is happening?"

Once again, the only response came with the repositioning of lips on lips. It could not have even been called a kiss as Vladimir only pushed his face against the other's. Guessing that the guard had never performed or received a kiss be-fore, Boris tried to pucker his lips. Vladimir responded in kind and the two of them stood, grappling each other and having a proper first kiss that lasted almost two minutes.

By this time, both men's bodies had responded to the inti-macy, and Vladimir lifted his friend, placing him somewhat brusquely on the mattress. Boris began to slip the kaftan off Vladimir as the kissing continued. After a few minutes of not being able to come up for air, the chef broke away and caught his breath. The two of them stared into each other's eyes, and Vladimir brought his hand to the back of Boris's head and pulled him in for more kissing. This time Boris re-laxed his jaw a bit and began testing Vladimir's lips with his tongue.

The guard continued to moan and pant as they kissed. Boris started to pull off his nightshirt, and Vladimir followed by removing his own underclothing. Again, they just stared for a frozen moment before hugging some more, now skin-to-skin. Boris moved to the mattress and pulled Vladimir alongside him.

They lay side-by-side on the bed holding each other. Hips ground together in a primal pelvic dance while the intensi-fied kissing continued. A minute later, Vladimir cried out in a crescendo as his body convulsed rhythmically. Boris could sense a moistened area around his navel, and he moved a hand in-between them.

"Oh, my, Vovka!" Boris panted, "It must have been a very long while for you."

The guard continued panting, "A long while for what?"

"Since your last pleasuring." Boris pulled Vladimir close.

"Pleasuring?" He panted. "I am not understanding what you're trying to say, Borushka."

Boris leaned back again so that he could see the other's face. "Have you never…? Oh, my goodness. You have never experienced the pleasure before."

"Pleasure? What pleasure?"

He clasped one of Vladimir's hands and placed it over the damp area between them. "Have you not found your underclothes damp like this in the morning before? Did it not feel wonderful a moment ago? More wonderful than you have ever felt?"

"Yes, it felt wonderful. Being with you is wonderful." His face appeared blank. "I have heard other fellows in the barracks talking about such matters, but I did not realize pleasure would be involved. The way they spoke made it sound more like combat."

"Here," and Boris placed Vladimir's hand on his own rigid, still-unfulfilled organ, "rub me, please."

"I am not sure what that will accomplish."

"Please, just move your hand up and down and in a minute or so you will understand. I assure you."

Vladimir began to stroke Boris tentatively and apprehensively. The chef stared into the artic-blue eyes and moaned. "Please kiss me again," he gasped.

As their lips met once more, Boris ejaculated, and Vladimir pulled his hand away swiftly. "What was that?"

After Boris regained his composure, he looked up at Vladimir through half-closed eyes. "I am now realizing that you have never been with another man before."

"I have never been with another person before. Is that bad? Is that wrong?"

"No. No." He hugged Vladmir tightly and kissed him on the side of the neck. "Oh, Vovka, it just seems there are a few things I will have to explain."

"I am sorry I made you wait so long, Borushka," and he turned away, eyes lowered, "but I had worried that you might not find me suitable because you had so much more experience with these things than I did."

"Experience?" coughed Boris. "That comes naturally with familiarity. Do you not have feelings for me?"

Vladimir's eyes grew frosty. "Do you not think I would sleep on this floor for all these months if I did not have such feelings?" Then he stared into Boris's eyes. "And you? I presume you have similar feelings toward me perhaps?" He then turned away and looked down.

Boris took the guard's chin and pulled his face so that they could look directly into each other's eyes. "Vovka, from the moment I saw you in the kitchen I knew that I wanted to be with you." He lowered his gaze. "I feel a bit silly telling you this now, but I even wrote our names in the dust from the blast on the table and realized how they fit together. Boris," with one finger he traced the letters on Vladimir's lightly-furred chest as he said the names, "Vladimir–Borimir."

"Borimir? What a queer-sounding word."

"Perhaps, but I found it fascinating nonetheless." Boris looked down at the bloodied clothing. The stains had spread from Vladimir to his own clothes and body during their clumsy attempt at love-making. "Please tell me what horrible thing has happened."

Vladimir adjusted himself so that he was sitting up. He hugged Boris and began to weep again. "Oh, Borushka," he whispered into the other's ear, "the most horrible thing. Someone threw a bomb at His Imperial Majesty and it blew off his legs." He started sobbing.

"Oh, Vovka." Boris held his lover tightly while the weeping and moaning continued. "I know he was quite fond of you, and you of him." Vladimir nodded. "How horrible to stand by and watch such an abomination. Is His Highness still with us?" Vladimir shook his head slowly and the crying increased. "Oh, my." He moved his hands around with comforting hugs but then stopped abruptly. "Is this blood from…?" Vladimir nodded.

"Perhaps we should get cleaned up," Boris suggested as he started to stand while Vladimir remained sobbing on the mattress. "I had waited so long to share this bed with you, but such sadness to know the reason for its occurrence." He glanced toward the door and saw something on the floor. Someone had slipped a message underneath during their intimacy. Boris picked it up and read the address, "Messieurs V.Y. Orlov & B.M. Zelany." He examined the wax seal of the Tsesarevich, Alexander Alexandrovich. "Vovka, we have received something very important." He waved the folded paper until it caught Vladimir's attention.

"Well, open it and read, please." He began collecting his various pieces of clothing while Boris read.

"I request an audience with you in the morning to discuss your services with the House of Romanov. Please attend me promptly at 9:00 in the Tsar's private rooms. P.I. Volk, Imperial House Minister." Boris looked over at Vladimir. "Vovka, do you know a P.I. Volk? That name is unfamiliar to me."

Vladimir shook his head as he continued to assemble his outfit.

"Our services? I hope the new Tsar is not planning to dismiss us. You are a favorite of his father, and I am a favorite of one of his brothers."

"You never know," Vladimir spoke with a hint of uncertainty. "I have heard that when the leaders change, the household changes too." His blank face portrayed the numbness from the day's horrific events.

Boris suddenly turned to Vladimir. "I wonder why 'His Little Highness,' Dmitri Konstantinovich himself–the cheap teapot–did not come knocking at our door. It seems he likes to take every advantage to peek in on us."

The guard snapped out of his anguish, "I believe he might be quite distraught at this time. I witnessed him running up to the sleigh carrying us from the scene of the attack, and he looked upon His Imperial Majesty in a very distressing state." The blank look returned.

Boris raised his eyebrows. "I suppose we will have to wait until the morning to know our fate, Vovka." He gazed at the motionless guard. "However, given our current placement,

I doubt either of us would have any difficulty obtaining suitable employment elsewhere. I, for one, am not worried, but I am quite hungry and suggest we stop at the kitchen after we clean ourselves. Yes? I can prepare us something nourishing."

Vladimir looked at Boris, nodded his consent. The two of them threw on their robes and proceeded to the bathing room together.

В. Н. Улов
Б. М. Залкий

Я прошу аудиенции у вас утром, чтобы обсудить ваши узы с Домом Романовых. Пожалуйста, послушать меня ровно в 9:00 в гостиных комнат Царских.

П. И. Волк,
Императорский Дом-министр

Palace staff lowered the Tsar's flag mid-afternoon. Church bells rang out, but this time their message signaled the disheartening death of Alexander II, His Imperial Majesty of Russia for 26 years. Darkness descended upon the storybook city of St. Petersburg as another of its rulers succumbed to the precarious upheaval of circumstance. Only a few streetlamps illuminated the gloomy lanes of the city. People prayed, lit candles in front of their holy icons and wailed privately in their homes or attended one of the myriad memorial masses. The man who had modernized their nation more than any ruler since Peter the Great had been taken from them.

позже

"Thank you for making food for just the two of us," Vladimir said as they returned to their suite with fresh bedclothes. The meal appeared to have revived his grief-stricken spirit. "You are quite the good cook!"

"Well… thank you!" Boris accepted the compliment. "I did train in Paris, after all."

"I just wish I could have enjoyed it without thinking back on the events of the day. The images still plague me." He closed his eyes and shuddered.

Boris touched his lover's arm gently. "This will take some time, but we shall get through it together."

"Yes. You take such good care of me. And dinner by candle. What a treat!" He began replacing the soiled sheets with the clean ones.

"I find it quite romantic." He beamed at Vladimir affectionately.

"Borushka," Vladimir paused the bed-making work, glanced at his partner and then continued, "Please keep in mind that this is all very new to me. I was raised with soldiers and serve His Imperial Majesty," he sniffled, "or at least did serve him."

"What is it you are trying to say, Vovka?"

"Well… you know… and you are the Kitchen Chief –"

"*Chef de cuisine, s'il vous plaît.*"

"Yes, yes, as you wish." He finished setting the clean sheets. "It's just that we need to be careful about our interactions in front of people. If others know about us, they may treat us differently."

"Vovka, we have slept together in this very room for many months now. I would wager that you and I are the only ones who truly believe you actually sleep on this floor. From what scuttlebutt I have heard, the rest of the staff think we are a married couple."

Vladimir looked down at the piles of bloodied bedclothes on the floor. "I see. Then I guess it is me who needs to adjust his attitude to the rest, not the other way round."

"You could say that, I suppose," Boris placed a hand on his partner's arm. Vladimir looked into his eyes and made a peckish attempt at a kiss.

"Is that how it is done?"

Boris smiled and hugged Vladimir. He then applied a proper kiss. A loving kiss. A kiss of longing and passion. "I have some more things to show you." He spread Vladimir's gown, knelt down and took his partner into his mouth.

"Borushka! How can you –?"

"Shush!" And he went back to suckling.

Vladimir began to moan and tremble. "Yes! Oh, yes! Oh! Oh!"

Boris stood and removed his own gown stepping to the freshly-made bed and guiding Vladimir by hand. He positioned himself on his back at the edge of the mattress to receive his partner. "And now, my love, here is what I have been waiting to share with you." He pulled the other's hips into his, guiding the saliva-moistened erection in.

"Oh! Oh!" They both cried, one in pleasure, the other in slight pain.

"Now, move yourself in and out."

"Am I not hurting you?"

"Not at all! Quite the opposite, I assure you."

"But you sounded like you were in pain."

"Only for the briefest moment, *mon cher*. Now, do as I told you."

Vladimir began, slowly at first, thrusting forward and back. "Mmmmm," he crooned.

"Yes!" Boris encouraged.

The plunges accelerated and Vladimir started moaning loudly. He stopped the movement and covered his mouth with one hand. Boris looked up and winked.

"And this is pleasurable for you as well?"

"Yes!" Boris encouraged.

The thrusting started up again, and both men huffed and grunted in delight.

"Borushka?" The rising-pitch of his voice sounded trembly and pressured.

"Yes!" Boris encouraged. He pushed his hips toward his partner forcefully. Vladimir stopped thrusting, convulsed ecstatically, groaned softly and collapsed on top of Boris, who squirmed from side-to-side a bit and brought on his own reason for groaning.

Once the pleasure subsided, Boris kissed Vladimir's neck, as it was the closest part to his mouth. "Thank you, my dearest."

Without moving his head, Vladimir responded, "Thanks to you as well. I think I might learn to enjoy this."

Boris smiled and giggled. "I really hope so. Appetite comes with eating, so they say." He struggled to move out from under the weight of the tall soldier. "Do you think you might actually sleep with me here in the bed tonight?"

Vladimir went to stand but wobbled a bit. He steadied himself by holding onto the mattress. "Are there more wonderful things you wish to show me?"

"Yes!" Boris encouraged.

позже

The next morning, Boris woke up encircled by Vladimir's strong arms. They had fallen asleep together for the first time, and somehow during the night, the guard had wrapped his protective limbs about the chef. Boris smiled. Boris smiled for quite a few minutes before glancing at the bronze pocket watch set in the giltwood stand on the desk. The hour approached 8:30.

"Vovka!" he shouted, attempting to rouse his lover. "Vovka! We must prepare for our meeting."

Vladimir began to shift slightly and his eyelids parted. "Hmmmm?" He looked down and saw his arms around Boris. "Mmmmmmm," he crooned as he hugged and shook his partner side-to-side.

Boris struggled out of the hold and got to the floor. "We must get ready to meet that P.I. Volk fellow." He began searching through some of his clothes to find clean under-things. "I do not think you will be wearing the same uniform as yesterday. Do you have time to go to the barracks to get another?"

The guard had finally sat up on the mattress. His hands caressed the sheets. "This is so comfortable. Perhaps you will let me sleep with you again soon." He smiled playfully.

"Tonight!–if you are lucky, I suppose–but first we have to find out whether we still have positions here. Please, Vovka, get dressed."

Vladimir pushed himself off the bed with palpable reluctance. He tossed on the robe from the previous day and walked to the door. "You are correct. I will have to get a clean tunic. I shall return shortly."

He opened the door and walked out into the dark hallway. The curtains on the palace windows remained undrawn. People passed with downcast eyes. On some of the tables lining the walls, the staff had placed candles, icons of St. Peter and miniature portraits of the recently-deceased Tsar.

Despite the somber mood from His Imperial Majesty's passing, Vladimir smiled to himself, but as soon as someone walking past noticed the smile, it turned into the placid guard mask he usually wore while on duty.

Boris worked at untangling his curls and getting into the new suit he wore as *chef de cuisine*. By the time he had gotten fully dressed, Vladimir returned in uniform.

"There is a pervasive sad gloominess about the Palace," the guard reported.

Boris took in the vision of his lover in uniform, measured and precise. "Perhaps people are still in shock from yesterday's tragedy."

"Yes. That must be it. I was not yet born when the previous Tsar died. I do not know what protocol is in place." He studied Boris in the suit. "And your outfit looks very sharp. Those clothes fit quite well."

"The suit is a bit uncomfortable," he wriggled, "but I wish to make a good impression."

"Indeed. Shall we?"

The two walked along the gloomy corridors, and no one seemed to give them a glance. Vladimir's military boots clacked in cadence on the marble tiles. When they arrived at the private rooms of His Imperial Majesty, the door opened.

A head covered with long greying hair popped out. It was the mysterious man from the previous day who had handed the Tsesarevich–presumably now the Tsar–a stack of papers.

"Gentlemen. Pray step in. I am Pavel Ivanovich, the Imperial House Minister." He opened the door further and ushered Boris and Vladimir inside. "Thank you for attending me, as requested." He then sat at the small desk Tsar Alexander had used for his personal writing. Two Chippendale chairs stood nearby. "Sit. Please."

The two servants did as requested and waited for the older man in the black robes to speak. For a minute or so, Pavel Ivanovich merely gazed back and forth at their faces with his steely-grey eyes while slowly stroking his hairy chin.

"I have asked you two here because you have both been valuable servants in the House of Romanov, especially you, Vladimir Yuryevich. I have been told your family has served this House for generations. In addition, you also attended His Imperial Majesty after his mortal injuries and brought him back to this very room."

Vladimir nodded silently. The crumpled sheets still lay upon the bed nearby.

"And you, Boris Mikhailovich, while a recent addition, your reputation for culinary delights is quite impressive."

"Thank you, sir," Boris responded.

"It is a sad business, indeed, that the people His Imperial Majesty attempted to help were the very ones who took his life. Our agents have rounded up the culprits and they shall pay for their crimes," Pavel Ivanovich stated flatly, without emotion. "The new Tsar has appointed me his special assistant with the title Imperial House Minister. I can assure you it sounds more impressive that it actually is. Just think of me as the eyes, ears and mouth of Alexander Alexandrovich." He sniffed audibly and a bland smile moved his lips slightly.

Someone rapped on the door from the hallway. "Excuse me," the Minister said as he rose and went to the hall.

Vladimir and Boris turned to each other with raised eyebrows and uncertain expressions.

Pavel Ivanovich returned with some papers. He dropped them on the desk and sat. "Thank you for your patience. As you probably know, when a regime changes, the house staff frequently changes as well. This exalted set of rooms," he waved one hand about, "has become my office for the time being because–quite frankly–no one else wished to use them, given the tragic events."

Boris and Vladimir nodded together.

"And I know you most likely have concerns regarding your continued service here, and that is why I have asked you both in: to inform you of the changes we have decided to implement." He smiled again but in a way that only one side of his lips raised. "Permit me," Pavel Ivanovich turned to the side table and poured some kvass, golden and translucent, into one of the former Tsar's cut crystal sherry glasses. Without drinking any, he placed it on the desk. "It has come to my attention that the two of you have some kind of… I don't know what to call it. Would you say it is a special relationship?" Vladimir tensed and his head snapped to Boris, who continued to look directly at the Minister. "Please take note that the new Tsar and I have no understanding of such things but neither do we condemn them. As long as you both continue to perform the duties required of you to the best of your abilities, no one from this governance shall persecute you, but we do ask that you maintain the dignity and propriety bestowed upon you by the Crown."

The two men looked at Pavel Ivanovich and nodded cautiously.

Minister Volk turned his head slightly away, but kept his eyes on Boris and Vladimir, "However, keep in mind that your every move in public shall be closely scrutinized, and, at the first sign of impropriety…" he turned back to them again but shook his head slowly from side to side.

Boris and Vladimir looked at each other and swallowed nervously.

"Vladimir Yuryevich," the Minister turned to the guard, "as you are probably aware, your former Lieutenant did not escape the bomb blast yesterday, and in recognition of your superior service and personal attentions to the new Tsar's father," Vladimir swallowed nervously, "your rank has been elevated to that of an officer, and you will assume the vacated position, Lieutenant of the Royal Guards."

Vladimir stood, bowed and saluted the Minister. "Sir, if given the opportunity to serve the new Tsar, I shall make every attempt possible to maintain his safety, and that of the other members of his family." He bowed again and sat down.

"Your predecessor failed in his attempt to maintain the safety of his charge. May your service prove more adequate." Pavel Ivanovich squinted and displayed his half-smile again. "Here," the Minister handed him some folded pages displaying the new Tsar's seal. "Take these to the Regiment Chief's aide. He will provide you with your new uniform and assist you with setting up your office."

"Thank you, sir. God save the Tsar."

Pavel Ivanovich glanced at Vladimir with his head tilted at a slight angle, allowing the cascade of grey hair to dangle on one side. "*You* save the Tsar." He pointed a gangly finger at Vladimir. "I am certain your God is occupied with so many other things." He turned to the blond man. "And you, Boris Mikhailovich," the Minister's eyes now evaluating the chef's appearance, "shall be our new Chief-of-Staff."

"Chief-of-Staff? What about Dmitri Konstantinovich? That is his position."

"Not any longer," Pavel Ivanovich droned. "He came to speak with me last evening. He informed me that after seeing the decrepit condition of the Tsar's body in the sleigh, he could no longer adequately perform his duties, tendered his immediate resignation and recommended you as his replacement."

Boris shuddered at the thought. "Oh, my," he looked at Vladimir with surprise. "I cannot believe that Dmitri Konstantinovich has been so easily put off, and more so that he wanted me to be his replacement. He always seemed quite obvious with his dislike for me."

"Believe me, I made every attempt to convince him to remain, but after a while I accepted the sincerity of his protestation and his nomination for replacement. You apparently have training that the others lack, and he assured me of your suitability for this duty." The Minister turned to Vladimir. "Do you suppose he would prefer it if I appointed someone else?"

"No, no!" barked Boris. "I wholeheartedly accept. I accept!" He turned to the Minister and nodded."

"Of course, you will both have to sign loyalty oaths to the new Tsar, when they have been drawn up."

"Of course!" Boris volunteered, and the Minister startled at the abrupt response.

"Now, as far as sleeping arrangements, you are both welcome to the chambers of your predecessors." Pavel Ivanovich looked at each in turn. "However, as it turns out, those particular rooms are much smaller than the suite you currently occupy. I might suggest keeping your present, shared quarters.

Both Boris and Vladimir nodded in agreement.

"Lieutenant Orlov," the Minister said, and Vladimir perked at the sound of his new title, "your first assignment will be to oversee the transition to the Palace at Gatchina. The new Tsar does not want to remain here in the Winter Palace as it has too many black memories for him. Please draw up a plan by tomorrow evening, when we shall meet in this office again."

"Yes, Your Excellency."

"Please, there is no need for such formality between us, Lieutenant. You may refer to me as 'Minister' or Pavel Ivanovich, as you see fit.

"Yes, Minister Volk."

"And Boris Mikhailovich, as the new Chief-of-Staff, your first duty will be to select a replacement Kitchen Chief. Do you have a suitable candidate in mind?"

"Yes, Your... Minister, I do."

Pavel Ivanovich smiled his half-smile. "Good. Please inform the new Kitchen Chief that a proper family dinner is expected tomorrow evening to mark the passing of the Tsar's father. Perhaps you can assist with that as it is all so sudden."

"Yes, Minister Volk."

"Do you have any further questions?"

The new Chief-of-Staff shook his head, but Vladimir raised a finger. "Yes, sir, if I may. What of Princess Catherine?"

"Ah, Princess Catherine...," Pavel Ivanovich intoned. "She shall remain here and keep her private rooms. Shall I mention when I see her that you asked after her?"

"Yes, please. She... favored me with her attentions."

"I see," induced a little smile. "Well, that is all. You may return to your duties."

Boris and Vladimir stood and walked to the door.

"Oh, gentlemen," the Minister called out, "I almost forgot. A toast." He stood and brought the small piece of stemware with him. After taking a delicate sip of the kvass, he shouted, "Long live the Tsar!" and he handed the glass to Vladimir.

The new Lieutenant swallowed a mouthful and shouted, "Long live the Tsar!" and handed the glass to Boris.

The new Chief-of-Staff took the kvass, looked at Vladimir, then at Pavel Ivanovich. He emptied the glass and shouted, "Long live the Tsar!" and handed it back to the Minister.

Pavel Ivanovich studied the crystal object with some curiosity, walked to the fireplace hurled the sherry glass into the recess, and it exploded in a flurry of shards. "Long live the Tsar," he whispered.

As they walked hurriedly along the corridor back to their room, Boris erupted, "Rank Six! I shall be Rank Six of Twelve!" His infectious smile bringing light to the darkened walkway. "What do you think of that, *Lieutenant?*"

Vladimir glanced sideways as they scurried along, "Your mother is going to be so very proud of you."

"Oh, yes! I must write her as soon as we get back to our room."

"Yes, Borushka, you must! And please–if you can remember, that is–let her know of my good fortune as well."

Boris laughed out loud and everyone within earshot turned to see who was so happy at a time of such sorrow. Vladimir grabbed Boris's hands and presented a solemn face to discourage any further frivolity.

When they returned to their room, Boris raced in and Vladimir closed the door behind him. They stood for a few moments just looking into each other's eyes.

"Such wonderful things, Vovka." Boris hugged his partner tightly. "May I have the honor of this dance?" He stepped back and held his hand out as if in the grand ballroom, a long line of dapper gentlemen awaiting such an invitation.

Vladimir frowned. "Dance? There is no music playing. Are you hearing things?"

Boris ignored the question, stepped closer, placed one hand on Vladimir's shoulder and the other around his waist. He began moving them in rhythm, as if an unseen orchestra provided the waltz.

"You are quite giddy for such dark times, Borushka."

Vladimir moved awkwardly like a Russian bear at first, but he eventually succumbed to the joyous moment, positioned his hands accordingly and swayed with Boris to the strains of the silent strings.

"I love you, Lieutenant Vladimir Yuryevich Orlov," Boris whispered as he careered his partner around the room.

"And I, uh…," Vladimir stammered, "um… love… you, Chief-of-Staff Boris Mikhailovich Zelany."

The two continued to move in rhythm throughout their private dance hall, smiling, for nearly a half hour.

Change brings both good and ill. Advancement brings new joys and responsibilities. Tides rise and fall, the sun rises and sets, the moon waxes and wanes, flowers bloom and wilt. None of us could know for certain what the next year, month, day, hour or minute could bring. All we have is hope.

---

[12] A city in southeast Ukraine where Cossacks drew up a reply to an ultimatum from the Turkish Sultan in 1676.

[13] Mishka is a diminutive form of Mihkail.

[14] "To arrive in Tula with one's own samovar" is the Russian equivalent to "Carrying coals to Newcastle."

[15] An informal circle of composers (Balakirev, Borodin, Cui, Mussorgsky, and Rimsky-Korsakov) who attempted to preserve the Slavic musical traditions rather than follow the evolving Western-European stylistic trends.

The second book of this series covers the period from 1881 to 1894. Tsar Alexander III had political views quite different from his more liberal father, and as ruler of Russia, he steered the ship of state in a different, and more austere, direction.

Boris and Vladimir continued to serve in their capacities, and they frequently interacted with the notable cultural artists of their time.

About the Author

WAYNE GOODMAN has lived in the San Francisco Bay Area most of his life (with too many cats). When not writing, he enjoys playing Gilded Age parlor music on the piano, with an emphasis on women, gay, and Black composers.

Also available, the book that developed from the author's interest in this time period.

Vanya Says, "Go!"
A Retelling of Mikhail Kuzmin's *Wings*

Wings was the first Russian-language novel to deal with same-sex relationships in a positive way. *Vanya Says, "Go!"* presents the story in a modern, more open way with an additional chapter.